INDEFENSIBLE

M A COMLEY

ACKNOWLEDGMENTS

Thank you as always to my rock, Jean, I'd be lost without you in my life.

Special thanks as always go to @studioenp for their superb cover design expertise.

My heartfelt thanks go to my wonderful editor Abby, my proofreaders Joseph, Barbara and Jacqueline for spotting all the lingering nits.

Thank you also to my amazing ARC group who help to keep me sane during this process.

To Mary, gone, but never forgotten. I hope you found the peace you were searching for my dear friend.

For Linda, one of my dearest friends and an inspiration throughout my career.

ALSO BY M A COMLEY

Blind Justice (Novella)

Cruel Justice (Book #1)

Mortal Justice (Novella)

Impeding Justice (Book #2)

Final Justice (Book #3)

Foul Justice (Book #4)

Guaranteed Justice (Book #5)

Ultimate Justice (Book #6)

Virtual Justice (Book #7)

Hostile Justice (Book #8)

Tortured Justice (Book #9)

Rough Justice (Book #10)

Dubious Justice (Book #11)

Calculated Justice (Book #12)

Twisted Justice (Book #13)

Justice at Christmas (Short Story)

Justice at Christmas 2 (novella)

Justice at Christmas 3 (novella)

Prime Justice (Book #14)

Heroic Justice (Book #15)

Shameful Justice (Book #16)

Immoral Justice (Book #17)

Toxic Justice (Book #18)

Overdue Justice (Book #19)

Killer Blow (DI Sara Ramsey #2)

The Dead Can't Speak (DI Sara Ramsey #3)

Deluded (DI Sara Ramsey #4)

The Murder Pact (DI Sara Ramsey #5)

Twisted Revenge (DI Sara Ramsey #6)

The Lies She Told (DI Sara Ramsey #7)

For The Love Of… (DI Sara Ramsey #8)

Run For Your Life (DI Sara Ramsey #9)

Cold Mercy (DI Sara Ramsey #10)

Sign of Evil (DI Sara Ramsey #11)

Indefensible (DI Sara Ramsey #12)

I Know The Truth (A psychological thriller)

She's Gone (A psychological thriller - coming August 2021)

The Caller (co-written with Tara Lyons)

Evil In Disguise – a novel based on True events

Deadly Act (Hero series novella)

Torn Apart (Hero series #1)

End Result (Hero series #2)

In Plain Sight (Hero Series #3)

Double Jeopardy (Hero Series #4)

Criminal Actions (Hero Series #5)

Regrets Mean Nothing (Hero #6)

Prowlers (Hero #7 Coming July 2021)

Sole Intention (Intention series #1)

Grave Intention (Intention series #2)

Devious Intention (Intention #3)

Merry Widow (A Lorne Simpkins short story)

It's A Dog's Life (A Lorne Simpkins short story)

Cozy Mystery Series

Murder at the Wedding

Murder at the Hotel .

Murder by the Sea

Death on the Coast (April 2021)

A Time To Heal (A Sweet Romance)

A Time For Change (A Sweet Romance)

High Spirits

The Temptation series (Romantic Suspense/New Adult Novellas)

Past Temptation

Lost Temptation

Tempting Christa (A billionaire romantic suspense co-authored by Tracie Delaney #1)

Avenging Christa (A billionaire romantic suspense co-authored by Tracie Delaney #2)

PROLOGUE

*K*eeping a safe distance, they watched and waited.

"How much longer do we have to wait? This is doin' my frigging head in."

"Patience. You know what youngsters are like, I doubt if she'll hang around too long."

The younger one, Adam, hunkered down in his seat and zipped up his hoodie. "Give me a nudge when you see any action."

He tutted and observed all that was taking place on the street through his mirrors, hating this time of the year; the nights were getting lighter and hampering their business.

His attention was drawn back to the bungalow ahead of them. He saw movement in the lounge and then two figures appeared at the front door. He elbowed his partner. "We're on. She's leaving."

Adam sat upright. His hoodie still in place, he fidgeted in his seat. "What are we waiting for? We need to make the move *now*."

Expelling an impatient breath, he glared at his partner. "What have I told you about being too hasty? Pace yourself, lad. At least, wait until her visitor has left. Hide your face, she's coming this way."

They both looked in the opposite direction until the young woman had passed, her pace quickening the closer she got to the main road.

They had kept the bungalow under observation for a while now, knew who the girl was and what she did after she paid her grandmother a visit. She'd be heading for the bus stop on the main road. That bus was due to arrive in two minutes.

"What now?" Adam demanded.

"We wait it out, until we're sure the granddaughter has got on the bus and is safely on her way back into town."

"I hate this!"

"That much is obvious. Think of the reward we're about to receive, that should put you in a good mood."

"You reckon? Nothing is guaranteed in our line of business, you know that."

It was true, but he'd been in this long enough to know these pensioners were ripe for the picking. *Always have a stash of cash hidden somewhere.* Most old folks detested putting their money in a bank, now that the banks were encouraging people to go over to online banking. He and his new partner had been making a killing lately, careful how they went about their business to avoid being captured by the police. So far it had worked out well, but he had always planned things methodically in the past—he regarded himself as a professional in his field. That was before he'd teamed up with his partner.

He jabbed a finger in his partner's thigh. "Come on, time to go. Remember what I said, keep your head down low. Take your hoodie off once we've reached her front door, though, got that? The last thing we want to do is make her suspicious."

"All right. You're beginning to sound like a broken record, repeating yourself over and over all the time." He jabbed a finger at his temple. "I ain't got shit for brains, no matter what you think."

Debatable at times. "Of course you haven't, I was only going over the plan—"

Adam slammed his fist on the car door. "Again! For the seven hundredth time."

"Slight exaggeration."

"All right, can we get on with this now?"

He swallowed down the acid which had lodged in his throat and

2

got out of the vehicle, pressing the key fob as he took a few steps towards the woman's house. He cautiously glanced over his shoulder, to check the coast was clear. They stepped onto the path that led up to the woman's front door.

After he rang the bell, he motioned for his partner to remove his hood and they both straightened their hair. "Ready? Don't go steaming in there, right? She seems a feisty one."

Adam grunted. "I'm going to leave it all to you, as planned."

The door opened and immediately closed to a couple of inches. The woman, already on guard, peered around it and demanded, "What do you want? I'm not buying anything."

"Hello, love. We noticed you've got a few slates missing on the roof. Hear me out, we're trying to do you a favour. We've stopped off and helped a few of the old dears on the street in need of assistance."

"Is that right? Well, my son happens to be a roofer and he gets up there to check it out regularly. So bugger off!" She began closing the door, but Adam thrust his foot in the way and shoved it open. The woman stumbled backwards into the hallway. "I'll scream if you don't leave this instant."

Adam raised his fist and threatened her. "Do that and you won't live to spend another Christmas with your family, Grandma."

"Oh my! What do you want? I don't want any trouble. My husband is on an errand, he'll be back soon. If he catches you here, there'll be trouble."

Adam took a pace forward, getting right in her face. "Don't bullshit us, we know you live alone. Where do you keep it?"

Her hand shook as she placed it on her cheek. "Keep what?"

"The money. Hand it over and we'll let you get on with your day."

"I don't have any. I'm a very poor pensioner. I'm telling you, he'll be back soon."

Adam gave the woman a backhander and knocked her to the floor. "We know you ain't got a husband, so stop lying to us."

"I do. He's gone out to the shops, he'll be back in a few minutes. Leave while you've still got the chance."

The older one remained with the woman while Adam took off,

searching her home. Drawers could be heard opening and banging shut again at the end of the long hallway. "It would be better if you told us where the money is, sweetheart. We don't mean you no harm."

"I won't. If I give it to you, then what am I supposed to live on? You need to both get a life, and more importantly, a job. Go on, jog on. If I get to my feet, I'm going to ring the police."

"We'll be out of your hair soon enough, providing you tell us where you keep your loot."

"Nope, it's not going to happen. Did I mention my other son is a copper? See that camera up there, he's watching my every move. I bet you didn't know that, did you?"

His head shot around to the equipment sitting on the wall and he laughed. "Nice try, old lady, that's a smoke detector, nothing more."

"It's a camera made to look like a smoke detector, *dimwit*. He'll be here soon, mark my words. Not all old folks are incapable of looking after themselves, you know. You've picked on the wrong pensioner this time."

Adam appeared at the end of the hallway with a bundle of notes in his hand. "Any more of the readies anywhere else, bitch?" he demanded.

"No. You put that money back, I've put it aside for my funeral. You take that and my family will have to bear the burden."

"Tough, it's ours now." Adam came towards them. "Is this all of it?"

"Yes, that's my life savings in your hands. *Mine,* not yours. Why don't you get a proper job instead of robbing elderly folks who have worked hard all their lives and have a pittance to show for it?"

Adam leaned down and sneered in her face. "This is so much easier than working for a living. Stop messing with me, lady, tell me where the rest of it is. I know you oldies prefer to scatter your funds around the house. Hand it over, or suffer the consequences."

"Hey, hurting her wasn't in the plan. Let's take what you've found and get out of here."

"What's the rush? I'm having fun. She's got more stashed away, I just know it. Hand it over, Grandma."

The woman held a hand up, guarding her face. "I haven't. I've told you, that's all I have. Take it and get out of my home."

"Ain't gonna happen. We're not in any rush. We'll stay here all night if we have to."

"Adam, come on. She's got a son in the police, let's get out of here."

Adam bent down again, his nose almost touching the old woman's. "Is that right? You wouldn't be trying to pull a fast one now, would you?"

"Me? No, I don't know what you're talking about. Ring the station and ask for Roger Purcell, he's my son."

"Nah, can't be arsed. The money, where is it?"

She sighed and squirmed away from him. "I haven't got any. That's all I have. Please, don't take it. Go now before my husband returns."

Adam knelt on one knee, getting ever closer to her. "Lies, lies, lies. We've been watching you for months, you haven't got a husband so don't lie."

"I... I have, he doesn't get out much. If you've been watching us, you might not have seen him."

Adam raised his fist and punched her in the face. Blood poured from her nose.

The older one yanked on Adam's arm. "Get up, leave her alone. We're out of here."

"Not going to happen until I get more money out of her. I know she's hiding it somewhere. Where is it, bitch?"

The old woman leaned back on her elbow, distancing herself from Adam. "I haven't, that's all I have. Why won't you believe me and leave?"

"Once a liar, always a liar. You ain't got no husband, but I believe you've got another stash of money somewhere, so give it up and we'll leave you in peace."

"You've broken my damn nose. Eighty-five years on this earth and no one has ever struck me like that. What gives you the right to bully me? To steal what is mine?"

"Hand it over or..." Adam drew a hand across his throat; his meaning was obvious to all three of them. "You want to die today?"

She trembled and her shoulders dipped as if defeated. Her voice shaking, she said, "What sort of question is that? Of course I don't, but I have no other money. I would tell you where it was if I did, I swear I would. Please, leave me alone, you've got what you want."

"We want more, this isn't going to keep us in beer for more than a few days."

"Beer money, is that what this is about? You're prepared to kill me for *beer* money? My Lord, I've never heard the like. Just go."

"Come on, Adam, you heard her, she hasn't got any more cash around here. Time's getting on, we need to be elsewhere."

Adam rose to his feet. His hand went behind him and came out holding a ten-inch kitchen knife.

"Wait! That wasn't part of the plan. Don't do it. Put it away, Adam. Now!"

"Shut the fuck up, old man. I ain't leaving here until she hands over all the cash she's got hidden in this crummy house. You hear me, lady?"

The old lady gasped, her gaze drawn to the knife in his outstretched hand. "Don't you think I would give you the money if I had any extra? I haven't, I swear. Please, leave me alone. Don't do this."

Adam tipped back his head and let out a demonic laugh. "Now she's scared, good and proper, but she's still not giving the money up. Your loss, lady. You've probably led a full life already, it's all downhill from now on, you're going to thank me for putting you out of the misery that lies ahead of you."

The older one grabbed Adam's arm. He could see the terror in the woman's eyes, almost pleading with him to intervene. "Adam, no! Leave her alone. I won't allow you to do this. She's done nothing wrong. She doesn't deserve to go out like this."

"Shut the fuck up. That's your problem, you're all talk and no action. Whereas I, always see a plan through to its conclusion."

"Your plan, not mine. I didn't want this to end like this. There's no reason to kill her, let her be."

"You're a wuss, always have been and always will be. Wusses never prosper in this life. Get out if you don't want to see it."

He stared on as Adam thrust the knife into the woman's chest, over and over until her screams died down and blood covered her white blouse and jumper.

Satisfied, Adam took the money and left the house. Regret coursed through the older man. *Why did I get him involved? Now I have the old woman's blood on my hands.*

1

"Before you go, ma'am, I've just received a call that I think you'll be interested in."

Sara stared at the desk sergeant and glanced up at the clock on the wall behind him. "At nine-fifteen on a Monday evening? When my beloved husband probably has my dinner waiting for me on the kitchen table? This better be good, Jeff."

He winced. "Sorry, I believe it's good enough to want to bypass your dinner."

She stepped closer, leaving her partner behind, and warned, "This better be worth it now that you've managed to grab my attention."

"We've had a call from a concerned neighbour. She popped out to the shops and when she came back, she found her elderly neighbour's door wide open and her lying in the hallway, dead. Looks like a suspicious death."

Sara held out her open hand. "Give us the address. As if I can turn an elderly victim down. Reminds me of the first case I was assigned when I joined the station. I've always been a sucker for the old and infirm."

He smiled and nodded. "That's what I thought. Here you go."

Sara looked at the address and ran through the map forming in her mind. "I know it, out near Callow, isn't it?"

Jeff nodded. "That's right, not far."

Sara turned and faced Carla. "Do you want to tag along or are you going to call it a night?"

"If I had a hot man waiting for me at home, I'd tell you to do one, as I don't, count me in."

Sara sniggered and pushed open the main door. "My car or two cars?"

"We might as well go in one car, you can drop me back here on your way home since you have to pass the door, anyway."

"You read my mind. Hop in." Sara inserted the postcode into the satnav and started the engine. While the machine calculated the route, she drove out of the car park in the direction of the crime scene.

"Just what we need at the end of a long day, eh?" Carla groaned.

"I was thinking the same. Inconsiderate bloody criminals. One of these days, we'll get home at a decent hour."

Carla laughed. "Umm... I think we do okay, compared to some of the officers working at other stations. Like I said, I'd feel peeved if I had a hot fella at home. I live in hope though."

Sara patted her partner on the knee. "You'll find someone special soon."

"I thought Gary was special, at the time. I suppose he was... until the accident happened."

Hearing his name caused Sara to revisit the last time she'd encountered the fireman. Her warning rattled the inside of her head.

"You okay?" Carla asked, interrupting her wayward thoughts.

"Yeah, sorry. In a world of my own there for a moment or two."

"Thinking about your own loved-up relationship and making comparisons?"

"No, not at all. Speaking of which, I'd better ring Mark and tell him I'm going to be late home." She punched in her husband's mobile number and spoke to him on the hands-free. "I'm in the car, say hello to Carla."

"Hi, Carla."

"Hi, Mark. Hope you're doing well?" Carla replied.

"Not bad. You?"

"Fine, thanks."

Sara coughed a little and said, "Sorry to break up the pleasant catch-up. You're going to hate me for what I'm about to say."

"Don't tell me, you've got to work later than anticipated."

She didn't detect any animosity in his tone, Mark wasn't the type. He was as easy-going as they came. "Sorry, hon. Yep. To be fair, we were on our way home when we received the call. I've got to attend. I hope you understand."

"Of course I do. As it happens, I've had an emergency call as well. A cat has been knocked down and is on the way to the surgery. I'm in the car now."

"Brilliant. No, that came out wrong. I meant I'm glad I'm not the only one who is spoiling the evening we'd planned."

He chuckled. "A take-away and a romcom on the box, it'll keep for another day. I'm at the surgery now. Give me a ring in a couple of hours, let me know how you're getting on and when to expect you home."

"I will. Good luck fixing the cat. Love you."

"Thanks. Love you too. Bye, Carla. Stay safe the pair of you."

"We will."

"Bye, Mark. Good luck with the pussy." Carla sniggered.

Sara hung up and blew out a relieved breath. "I'm so pleased he's going to be otherwise engaged. Hey, you haven't mentioned it, have you seen Gary around lately?"

"Nope. The less I see of him, the better. Couldn't cope with his mood swings a moment longer."

"You need to get out there, socialise a bit more and find another willing partner."

"Ain't going to happen when we get call-outs like this to attend, is it?"

Sara turned to look at her and shrugged before flicking her gaze back to the road ahead. "You're right. I did give you the option to back out."

"I know. Maybe if I had something better on offer, I would have turned you down."

Sara concentrated on her driving. Her eyes were tired, and she was having trouble adjusting to the dark now they were away from the city out on the country roads. She leaned forward, peering ahead over the steering wheel.

"Is something wrong?"

"I can't see a damn thing. I'm being extra vigilant in case the local wildlife makes a sprint across the road."

"Get to Specsavers. You're turning me into a nervous passenger."

"Crikey, they're not that bad."

"Aren't they? How come I can see perfectly well then?"

Sara growled. "I'm beginning to wish you'd brought your own car."

"You're not alone," Carla chuckled.

Five minutes later, they pulled into a street filled with a couple of patrol cars, a few SOCO vans and a crowd of onlookers to boot. "Jesus, haven't these people got anything better to do? It's at times like this I pray for it to piss down, they'd soon lose interest and trundle off home."

"You're off on one." Carla shook her head. "It's called human nature when people are curious."

"Curious or nosy parkers tend to blight my life. I can't stand them, there, I've said it." Sara sighed. "Come on, let's get suited up. Will you get the team organised? Ensure they shift these buggers back and push the cordon out further? I have a feeling the press will already be on their way."

"Leave it to me."

They left the car and grabbed a couple of white paper suits and a set of blue shoe coverings each then separated before they reached the house. Sara poked her head over the threshold and found Lorraine, the pathologist, crouched down, examining the victim.

"How's it going? I don't suppose you have any information for me yet, do you?"

Lorraine glanced up, her eyes watering. "I'm glad you're here. This case needs to be handled sensitively."

"All cases should be handled sensitively, in my opinion, Lorraine. What's different about this one? Are you all right?" Lorraine stood up and walked away from the corpse. On the other side of the hallway, she withdrew a tissue from inside her suit and blew her nose. Sara moved closer to the woman who had become a good friend to her since her arrival in Hereford. "What's wrong, matey?"

Lorraine stood there, staring at the victim for a while and then whispered, "She's someone's mother, grandmother even, and she looks… just like my grandmother."

Sara rubbed Lorraine's arm, rustling the paper suit. "I'm so very sorry. What else can I say?"

"Nothing. I need to buck my ideas up, pull myself together. Pronto. And usually, it's not a problem, but this time, I have to admit, I'm struggling."

"We all get times like that. Lord knows I've had a fair few over the years, with what happened to Philip."

"Ouch, I never thought of that. I'm sorry, I feel stupid now." Lorraine paced the area.

"Don't be. We wouldn't be human if some of the shit we had to contend with didn't affect us personally. Why don't you hand the case over to someone else?"

The pathologist played with the zipper on her suit for a few seconds, lost in thought. "Nope, it's not going to happen. Your kick up the backside should be enough to put me on the right track again. I apologise for my lack of professionalism."

"Don't you dare say that. You're here, attending the scene and doing what you do best, aren't you?"

"Barely. But I'll be back to normal in a second or two."

Sara inclined her head. "Want me to give you some space?"

"No, I'm fine. You'll be wanting to get home to Mark."

"Don't worry about that. I'm here for the duration, Lorraine." They both took a few paces back towards the victim and surveyed the body. "Seems like overkill to me."

Lorraine sighed. "You could say that. She's in her eighties for fuck's sake, hardly a threat, is she? And yet, here she lies, bloody as hell. A quick assessment and I found at least twenty stab wounds to her chest. I'm thinking one or two would have been enough to have killed her, so why the excess?"

"You believe she knew the killer?"

"Usually that's the case. Or we could be looking at someone with anger issues. Stating the obvious, I know, but you get where I'm coming from."

"I do. Could it be a burglary gone wrong and the perp got frustrated with her?"

"At this stage, anything and everything is possible."

"What about the family? Did she live alone or do we know if anyone else lives here with her?"

"I had a brief chat with the neighbour who rang nine-nine-nine. She said the victim lived alone but had frequent visits from her family members."

"I'll have a chat with her, maybe she can give us some contact information for them."

Lorraine pointed at a console table halfway down the hallway. "Address book on there, or maybe look through the call list on the phone at the recent calls coming in."

"Good thinking, I'll do that. Are you okay now?"

"I'm getting there. I'll be all right as long as I don't look at her face."

"Makes sense. I'll have a chat with the neighbour first. Which side?"

"On the right. Marjorie Fellows. I've told her to expect someone, didn't realise you'd still be on duty at this time of night."

"It's not such a shock to the system these days. They're expecting us to do more and more work even though they're intent on cutting the hours."

"Bugger, how is that fair?"

"You tell me. I've got a tough decision to make soon. I've put it off as long as possible." Sara lowered her voice and glanced up at the doorway on the lookout for her partner. "They're telling me I have to make cuts. Give a team member the big heave-ho."

"Shit! I don't relish the task you have ahead of you. Do you have anyone in mind?"

"That's just it, no, I haven't got a clue. I have a sensational team, not one of them is a prankster or is guilty of not pulling their weight on an investigation. So how the fuck am I supposed to choose?"

"Does Carla know?"

"Negative. I can't share that sort of news, damn, I shouldn't be telling you this. The burden is laying heavily on my shoulders, though."

"Damn. I'd hate to be in your shoes, that's a nightmare scenario to have to deal with."

Sara motioned with her head at the corpse below them. "Some issues are easier than others to handle in this life, although it might not seem that way at the time."

"You'll work around it, if that's what you have to do."

"I hope so. I'll be back in a few minutes. Tell Carla where I am if I don't see her first."

"I will. Good luck."

Sara left the house and searched the immediate area for Carla. Her partner was having an animated conversation with one of the onlookers. She decided to leave her partner to deal with the problem and to go next door to the neighbour.

After ringing the bell, she stepped back. A worried looking woman opened the door a fraction.

Sara flashed her ID. "Mrs Fellows, I'm DI Sara Ramsey. Would it be possible to step inside to have a brief chat with you?"

"Yes, yes, come in out of the cold. I've been expecting you."

Mrs Fellows opened the door wider and allowed Sara access to the house. A small dog charged at her and the woman raised her walking stick, blocking the dog in its path. "I wouldn't hit him with it, it's just a deterrent, he's territorial and often goes to bite strangers. Once he's used to you, he'll be fine. I'll lead the way into the lounge, he'll get in his basket once you're sitting down. You're not scared of him, are you? I can put him in the kitchen if you're feeling uncomfortable."

"Don't shut him away on my account. If you think he'll settle down, I'll take my chances with him."

"Come through. I'd offer you a cup of tea, but I only have enough milk for some cereals in the morning."

"You don't have to do that for me."

"I don't get many visitors nowadays, so what's the point in getting in extra shopping just in case."

"I understand that. Don't your family visit you?"

"No, not now the money has run out. My husband had a lot of debts I didn't know about. When he died, I was forced to pay them off. This place is rented. I had to sell the house. The kids blamed me for selling off their inheritance, and that's it! I'm dead in their eyes. Oh dear, I shouldn't say that, not with what has happened next door. Poor Val, she was such a lovely lady."

"I'm sorry to hear that. It's hard dealing with families through life's tough times, such as when a parent dies. I hope you manage to get in touch with them to sort things out soon."

"No chance of that happening, not with my family. Selfish fuckers, the lot of them. I barely have two pounds to my name and they couldn't care less. Val used to see me right, cook meals for me when I couldn't afford to feed myself. Now she's gone, well, I imagine I won't be long behind her."

Tears pricked Sara's eyes and a large lump formed in her throat. "That's tough. Maybe Age Concern can be of some help, or some other charity in the area."

Mrs Fellows batted the suggestion away with her hand. "I can't be bothered. I have my pride, that keeps me going most days."

"It needn't be like that. Do you want me to have a word with someone? I'll willingly do it for you. You shouldn't go hungry."

"You're very kind. I sense you're going to have enough on your plate trying to find the bastard who did that to Val." She reached for a tissue from the packet on the coffee table. "I'm sorry, here I go again. I've done nothing but cry since I got back home. I'll never get rid of the image of her lying there with her eyes open. It was such a shock."

"I'm sure. Thank you for plucking up the courage to dial nine-nine-nine."

"Of course." She gasped. "Not sure how her family will take it. If I'd had Hazel's number, I would have called her. I think she gave it to me years ago, but like everything around here, it soon got lost. I'm not one for putting things away safely. I usually write things on a scrap of paper and it tends to end up in the bin a few weeks later."

"Don't worry. I'm sure we'll be able to locate her soon. Any idea which area Hazel lives in?"

"In the city somewhere. I'm hopeless, can't give you more than that, I'm afraid."

"Her surname?"

"Val's was Purcell, but Hazel is married to Ray. I can't, for the life of me, think what their surname is. I feel such a failure. I should have been more careful and jotted their number down in a book somewhere. Mind you, I probably would have thrown that out sooner or later as well."

"Don't beat yourself up. I'll get on to the station, see what they can tell me. I'll be right back." She moved from her seat and the monster dog ran out of his bed and nipped her heel before his owner could intervene. "Hey you. I'm friend, not foe."

"Toby, get back. How dare you do that? Want to get put down for biting a police officer, do you?" Mrs Fellows shouted.

The dog ran back to its bed with its tail between its legs.

"It's fine, no harm done." Sara continued into the hallway and rang the station. "Jeff, it's me. Do me a favour and try to find a next of kin for me for Val Purcell."

"Ah, I was just about to ring you, ma'am."

"You were? About what?"

"I have her next of kin standing in front of me."

"That's great news. Isn't it?"

"Depends on how you look at it. Roger Purcell works at the station. He's a DS, ma'am."

"Holy crap. Does he know?"

"Yes, he's in shock. I've arranged for a car to come and collect him. He'll be on his way to you shortly."

"Ugh… okay. Thanks for the heads-up, Jeff. How is he?"

"As well as can be expected."

"Okay. I'll wait at the house. I'll make sure the pathologist finishes with his mum soon, before he arrives."

"Thanks, I'm sure that will help, ma'am."

Sara ended the call and returned to the living room. Mrs Fellows was holding her stick out to deter the devil dog from attacking her a second time.

"Hello, dear, how did you get on?"

"Very well. Mrs Purcell's son is on his way here. So, if you'll excuse me, I have to go and inform the pathologist of his imminent arrival."

"Of course. Will you be back?"

Sara smiled, trying to put the woman at ease. "I'm not sure. Rather than leaving you on tenterhooks, why don't I send a uniformed officer in to take down your statement? Ordinarily I would do it, but it's imperative I speak to Val's son as soon as he gets here."

"I understand completely. That poor lad. Does he know?"

She nodded. "Yes. Thank you again for putting in the call so quickly, it could have a massive effect on the investigation if we can get the word out on the street rapidly."

"That's a relief. I hope you find the person who robbed her of her life. Bang him up and throw the key in the bloody River Wye, that would be my advice."

"It would be tempting, believe me." Sara smiled and waved from the safe distance of the doorway. "Take care and please, in light of what's happened next door, promise me you'll stay vigilant at all times."

"I will. I doubt if anyone will come near the place, not with Toby guarding me."

"I can imagine. I'll leave a card by the front door, slip it into your purse and ring me if you're at all concerned about anything in the next few days, okay?"

"You're very kind. I'll do that, although I wouldn't want to be the one to hamper the investigation."

"I mean it. Anything at all. It was lovely meeting you, and Toby of course."

As soon as its name was mentioned, the fearless dog growled at Sara.

She let herself out and met up with Carla at the victim's front door. "Everything all right?"

"Yep, is there anything else you need me to do?"

"Get a uniformed officer to take down Marjorie Fellows' statement next door. Bad news is that the victim's son is on his way."

Carla inclined her head. "That's good news, surely."

"It would be usually, except he's one of us."

"Oh fuck!" Carla pointed at the corpse lying in the hallway. "He can't see her like that."

"Don't worry, I've already considered that. I'm going to ask Lorraine to get a wriggle on."

"I'll get the statement actioned and then start knocking on some doors, leave you to deal with the grieving son when he turns up."

"Thanks. I'd suggest you get out of your protective suit first."

Carla glanced down at the rustling suit and then back up at Sara. "Yeah, I had every intention of doing that. Good luck."

"You too. I hope the exercise proves helpful, although judging by what Mrs Fellows told me, I very much doubt it."

"We can but try."

Sara watched Carla head back to the car and slip off her suit before she entered the house again. "How are you getting on? Almost finished?"

Lorraine was crouching, examining the victim. She stood and joined Sara. "I think I'm about done. I was just doing a final on-site assessment."

"Good."

"Why the rush?" Lorraine queried.

Sara sighed and let out another long breath. "Her son is on his way."

"Christ, you work quickly. Glad you managed to track him down. I did take a peek at the phone and wrote down a few numbers for you in case your trip next door didn't bear any fruit."

Sara issued her a half-smile. "Her son is a copper. I need you to get her out of here before he steps foot in the place. I know I wouldn't want to see my mum lying there cut to ribbons."

"Shit! I'm on it. What a shock for him."

"Definitely. I'll wait outside while you organise your team."

"We'll be done in five minutes max, I promise. He won't see her, not like this, not if I have my way." She turned away from Sara and shouted instructions to her team. One of them ran past Sara out to the van and returned carrying a zipped body bag.

Sara paced the doorway, glancing over her shoulder at the tender way Lorraine was treating the corpse in spite of her need to carry out the task swiftly. The zipper sounded as a car drew to a screeching halt at the edge of the cordon.

A man Sara recognised from the station dipped under the cordon but was stopped by one of the uniformed officers. Val's son lashed out and shouted, "That's my fucking mother in there, let me through or I'll report you."

Sara trotted over to the scene and stretched out her hand for him to shake. "Roger, I'm DI Sara Ramsey, please, try to keep your temper in check."

"I can do without the advice. I have as much right to be here as you do."

"Actually, you don't. But I agreed to you coming here. The pathologist is about to move your mother, will you be okay with that?"

"Of course I will. I want to see her."

Sara shook her head slowly. "I promise you, you wouldn't want to see her, not the way she is. Let the pathologist and her team clean your mother up first."

He took a few steps towards the house and stopped dead in his tracks. The front door opened and two of Lorraine's team carried the body bag out and placed it in the back of one of the vans.

Sara stared at Roger, gauging his reaction. He watched in disbelief and rocked back and forth on his feet as if tempted to push past Sara to get to his mother before rethinking the notion.

"Do you want to sit in the car and discuss this?" Sara suggested, placing a hand on his forearm.

"No. I want to see her." His gaze never left the van.

"Roger, you can't, you know the procedures where a victim of a violent crime is concerned."

He buried his head in his hands and crumbled before her eyes. Sara's gaze darted around the crowd for Carla. Where was her partner when she needed her the most? She spotted her over the other side of the road, talking to one of the neighbours, seemingly oblivious to what Sara was dealing with. She flung an awkward arm around Roger's shoulders and tried to coerce him back to his vehicle. He stood his ground, his hands now down by his side, staring at the van again.

"I can't believe she's dead," he whispered. His shoulders trembled with emotion under Sara's grasp.

"I know. Come on, let's get you in the car." She swivelled him and thankfully, he didn't put up a fight. They reached the squad car and Sara opened the back door. She placed a hand over his head, shielding it from the roof of the car, and then ran around the other side and got in the back beside him. "Are you going to be all right?"

"I don't know, am I?" he retorted, turning to face her.

"It's tough to see. I know you probably don't want to hear this, but I know exactly what you're going through."

His eyes narrowed as if he didn't believe her. "Do you?"

"Yes, my brother was murdered recently and I was the one who found his body. That's why I didn't want you to see her. Please try and remember her the way she was."

He opened his mouth to speak, but the words failed to form. He pressed his lips together again and gulped.

She ploughed on, "I have to ask you a few questions, are you up to it?"

"If I have to. I want to find out what happened as much as you do." He gulped a few times.

"Has your mother mentioned recently if she's felt unsafe in her own home?"

He shook his head and said adamantly, "No. If she had, do you think she'd still be living here, alone? A member of my family visited her every day. My daughter came by after college this evening. She was well loved. I pleaded with her to come and live with us, but she was eager to maintain her independence and now… she's no longer with us. What happened to her? I have to know. I can take it, I'm stronger than I look."

"We believe it might have been a burglary gone wrong. Your mother was stabbed several times. If it's any consolation, the pathologist reckons she would have died after the first couple of stabs."

"Hearing that is no consolation at all."

"I'm sorry."

"What do you propose doing about this, Inspector? Did any of the neighbours see anything? Who called it in?" His gaze flitted around at the houses nearby.

"The neighbour next door, Mrs Fellows. She was passing the house and saw the door ajar and your mother lying in the hallway. She dialled nine-nine-nine right away."

"Is she all right? The neighbour, I mean. She's a bit frail from what my mother told me. She used to look after her, take her meals et cetera."

"Marjorie's fine. Very shaken up, but otherwise, she's doing okay."

"I can't believe she's gone. My heart is split in two. My wife and daughter are going to be devastated when I tell them the news. Oh God, and my sister." He shook his head. The pain, anger and shock written on his face.

"Did your sister visit your mother often too?"

He nodded. "Hazel used to visit her regularly, yes. We all played our part after Dad died." He looked back at the van his mother had been put into as the vehicle left. Sara saw him grit his teeth; the muscle in his jaw ticked dangerously. "Who would do such a callous thing to a pensioner?" he roared a moment later, but before she could utter a word his anger subsided as the pain emerged once more. He sighed. "No, you don't have to answer that, we're all aware of the type of criminals we're dealing with on a daily basis. Fucking bastards. Sick fuckers if they get their kicks out of killing frail, defenceless OAPs." His hands covered his face again and Sara sat quietly as he shed yet more heartrending tears.

After a little while, she asked, "Are you okay now?"

"I fear I'll never be okay again. We only lost Dad last year to pancreatic cancer, and now I'll be burying Mum next to him. I thought we'd have her with us for another twenty years or more. I can't fathom any of this out."

"I understand," Sara offered. It was the only thing she could think of saying.

"My heart is broken beyond words. It's going to be a darn sight worse when I have to tell my wife and daughter, they loved her as much as I did." He shook his head again. His hands trembled and he balled them into fists, then he struck out at the front seat ahead of him, over and over again. Sara let him vent his anger, her own heart aching. "Jesus, what a frigging world we live in if a pensioner isn't safe in her own home. What type of shits are people breeding these days? Don't tell me this is down to drugs either. Druggies are the pits in my eyes. Lowest of the low, who have no one else to blame but themselves for getting into such a mess. I'm rambling now, I need to vent. I'm sorry for bending your ear like this. You need to get on with the investigation and I'm holding you up."

"Don't think that. You, of all people, know how these things work. My partner is out there doing a grand job, it's not as if it's a waste of time me being here with you."

"But the criminal has got away. What if he's out there, watching, pretending to be one of the rubberneckers?" He turned and surveyed the crowd surrounding the area, his eyes narrowing as if sizing up each of the onlookers individually.

"It's highly unlikely. I've been keeping an eye on the crowd and no one has stood out so far."

"He or she could be a good actor. You never know."

Sara doubted that was the case, but she agreed with him neverthe-less. It's the type of thing one did in the circumstances—agreed with the grieving relatives on certain aspects. "You might be right."

He faced her, looked her in the eye and asked, "When will I be able to see her?"

"Lorraine, sorry, the pathologist, will be in touch as soon as she's performed the... post-mortem."

He shuddered beside her. "Never thought a member of my family would ever be subjected to one of those damn things."

"I know it's hard to handle, but you're going to need to remain strong for your family's sake. Would you like me to ring your sister?"

"No. I'd rather do that myself. Hazel is going to be..." He trailed off with a deep sigh. "I'm going to miss Mum so much. We all are. I know we all say it, but truly, Mum was one in a million. I don't think we've ever had a cross word. There aren't many people who can say that about their parents, are there?"

Sara smiled. "No, not many. Why don't you go home to be with your family? There's nothing you can do here. SOCO will conduct a thorough search, let's let them get on with the job in hand. They'll be in touch should they need any information from you in the near future."

"I want to go, but something is telling me I should be here. I'm so confused as to what to do for the best. I've finished work for the day so my wife will be expecting me home around now. I don't want to tell her. This is going to break her heart. She lost her own mother around five years ago. She loved Mum so much, and now they're both gone. How unfair this life can be at times. Why are we all here to go out in such a despicable way?"

"So many questions, you're bound to have dozens of them. I'm so sorry, I just don't have all the answers for you. All I can tell you is that things will get better soon, I promise." Although Sara had mentioned her brother's death to Roger, she'd kept quiet about the other tragedy which had blighted her life several years before. The murder of her husband, Philip. Tears pricked as his image entered her mind. She swiped them away with the cuff of her jacket. This wasn't about her and the devastating traumas she'd had to endure. She was here to help Roger in his time of need.

"You mentioned your brother. I heard a rumour that it was your husband who got murdered. Daft things rumours, they always get twisted, don't they?"

Sara cleared her throat as unexpected tears surfaced. She glanced out of the window to look for Carla. All the time trying to think of a suitable response. "Ah, no, they're right. Losing my husband was one of the worst times in my life, but it's not going to help to compare notes, believe me."

"I get that. Thank you for being here, speaking to me like this. I appreciate it more than you realise."

She placed a hand on his arm and offered a weak smile. "We're work colleagues at the end of the day. I swear, you will get through this, with the love of your family. That's going to be paramount over the next few weeks. You should arrange time off from work. Would you like me to see to that for you? It'll ease your burden and allow you time to deal with your mother's funeral arrangements."

He ran a shaking hand through his hair. "Oh God. I can't do that. I'd break down every five minutes. Sandra will have to cover that side of things for me. She's more organised than me. More compassionate as well."

"Most women step up to the plate when things like this need to be dealt with. My door is always open should you need any advice, having gone through it myself in the past few months."

"Thank you, that's very kind of you, Inspector, but you haven't met my wife. She's regimented in everything she does. Methodical and an expert in many fields. She dealt with my father's funeral last year. I was thankful that she took over, it was too much for me and Mum to cope with at the time. Now we've got to do it all over again with Mum. Life is so cruel when you least expect it to be. I know death is inevitable, but to be bloody murdered..."

Sara patted the back of his hand again. "I know it's tough. You'll get through it. We're made of stern stuff, we police officers, right?"

"Sometimes," he muttered. Fresh tears tumbled onto his cheeks.

"Would you like me to drive you home?"

"No. I just want to sit here for a moment or two. Contemplate how I'm going to tell my family she's gone."

Sara let out a deep sigh. "I know you don't want to hear this right now, but you mentioned previously that your daughter dropped in to see your mother earlier. I'm going to need to speak with her, ask her if she saw anything. Do you think she'll be up to that?"

"Sonia is going to be distraught, but she'll realise the need to speak to you. She'll want this bastard caught ASAP before he or she can do it to anyone else."

"Good, you have her well trained by the sounds of it. I'll be in touch soon, give you a day or so to get your head around what's happened. Should Sonia want to speak to me sooner, here's my card. Just get in touch."

"Thanks. Speaking to you has dispersed the anger tearing me up inside."

"It gets easier. I know everyone spouts the same, but it's true. I'm going to get out there now and see what the neighbours have to say. Sit here a while and then go home. Wishing you well for what lies ahead. You've got this, you're stronger than you realise, we all are when our backs are against the wall."

He sniffed and wiped his nose on the sleeve of his jacket. "Again, I can't thank you enough for speaking to me. Laying things on the line for what lies ahead of us all has really helped. I'll stick around for five minutes longer, then make a move." He held his hand out in front of him, and it trembled a little. "I still need to calm down a bit first."

"Take all the time you need and for goodness' sake, ring me if you need any advice or want to run anything past me."

"Will you keep me informed about how the investigation is going?"

"If that's what you want, then yes. I want to assure you, you have Hereford's best team working your mother's case."

He smiled. "So I've heard."

Sara left the car and crossed the road to catch up with Carla who had just finished speaking to one of the neighbours. "Anything of use?"

"Nope. I've spoken to four people now. All of them have insisted they saw nothing."

"Damn. I find it incredibly hard to believe that no one on the street saw anything."

"In their defence, everyone I spoke to is a pensioner."

"Oh for a nosy beaked one in our midst," Sara said, her tone laced with sarcasm.

"I know. It is what it is, I suppose. Do you want me to keep at it?"

"No, let's leave it to uniform to carry out." She peeked over her shoulder at Val's bungalow. "I need to get back in there, see what SOCO have discovered, if anything. If nothing turns up, then I hate to say it, but I think we should call it a night and start afresh in the morning. I've already informed the next of kin."

"I agree. No point flogging a dead horse. Ouch! Sorry, not appropriate in the circumstances. How did the son take it? Or is that a stupid question?"

"He was in shock to begin with, but once it had sunk in, he was more concerned about how his wife and daughter would take the news. Apparently, either his wife or daughter visited his mother most days. His sister chipped in as well now and again. They obviously cared about her. His daughter was here earlier this evening."

"Bugger, glad she wasn't involved. Maybe whoever killed her grandmother was staking out the place and waited until the granddaughter left before they attempted to get in the house."

"Good point. If that's the case, then it's even more frustrating that no one saw anything, especially if the killer was possibly sitting out here for a while in their car."

Carla scanned the area all around her. "And no CCTV cameras in sight. We have an extremely canny killer on our hands."

"Yep, you read my thoughts there. Come on, I'll go back inside the house while you arrange for uniform to pick up where you left off, okay?"

"Gotcha."

They split up as they reached the path leading up to the bungalow. Sara eased open the front door to find Lorraine packing up her things ready to go. "How's it going?"

"I'm almost done here. How was the son?"

"Cut up, as you can imagine. He told me his daughter came to visit his mother earlier."

Lorraine gasped, her expression one of horror. "Oh God, I hope you're not suggesting that she had anything to do with this?"

Sara shook her head and smiled. "No, I didn't jump to that conclusion, although now you've mentioned it…"

"Shit! Forget I said anything," Lorraine mumbled, staring at the bloodstains in the hall carpet.

"Are you sure you're okay?"

Lorraine sniffled and stretched her neck, forcing her head up high. "Yep, I'll get there. It's going to be tough doing the PM on her."

"Do you have to? Can't you summon one of your colleagues to step in for you?"

"I don't want to be seen as a wuss. I'll leave her until the morning. Hopefully, I'll have got my head sorted out overnight."

Sara rubbed her arm. "I think you're wise leaving it for tonight, you look shattered, sweetie. A good night's sleep will be just what you need to help combat what lies ahead of you in the morning."

"If I manage to get to sleep. I don't think I've had eight hours for months now, damn insomnia."

"Oh no, I didn't realise you suffer from that. Have you seen a doctor? Maybe they can give you a course of tablets to take."

"No way. I refuse to get addicted to any pills they're likely to dish out. I've seen what those fuckers do to a person's insides, remember. The pills I'm referring to, not the doctors, although it amounts to the same thing. I've never been one for downing pills at the drop of a hat."

"I'm the same. I'm glad you didn't go into detail about the damaging effects. I used to have a relative, an aunt actually who constantly took her husband's tablets. Co-codamol, is it? She had a heart problem in a different country and was taken in for tests. I asked her if she'd told the docs she was taking her husband's tablets and she was flabbergasted at the suggestion. The docs released her after a few days, couldn't figure out what was wrong with her because she continued to lie to them."

"How terrible. Was she addicted to the drugs? Who in their right mind would take another person's prescription like that?"

"Beggars belief, right? Yes, I believe she got addicted to them. Anyway, she died a few months later and the PM revealed the damage the tablets had caused to her internal organs; they were in a dreadful state. The pathologist got in touch with Mum to ask if her sister had ever taken tablets in large quantities, and that's when the truth came out."

"Shocking. It's tales like those and what I see on a daily basis that is behind my decision to steer clear, even of paracetamols, can't stand the bloody things."

"I'm with you. I have to be desperate to pop a pill. Anyway, getting back to the murder. I need to know what SOCO found, if anything."

"Quite right, let's get back on track. Nothing much would be the answer. No forced entry and as the incident happened right by her front door, I think we can safely assume that she opened her door to her killer and he or she took advantage of the situation. The house was turned over slightly, maybe they were searching for money. Everyone believes the elderly keep funds in the house, don't they? That's nothing new, is it?"

"Yeah, that's true. The way banks are ripping us off with pitiful interest on our money, who can blame them? I need to get in touch with her family or Roger, see if they knew if she kept any money here or not. Maybe I'll leave that until the morning. All right if I take a snoop around?"

Lorraine shrugged. "Feel free. I'm out of here. I'll get the report back to you ASAP, it won't be for a few days though."

"I understand. I know you'll do your best for me."

"No question about that. Goodnight, Sara."

Sara tapped her friend on the arm and smiled. "You know where I am if you ever need to unburden yourself, don't you?"

"I do. You're a good person, Sara, don't ever let anyone tell you differently. Hereford is lucky to have you here."

Sara's cheeks warmed. "Thanks, I'm lucky to be here. Let's face it, we wouldn't have become friends if I hadn't moved away from Liverpool, and I would probably be a miserable widower if I hadn't bumped into Mark."

Lorraine laughed. "I'm a *miserable* spinster for my sins, but working hard to change that."

Sara winced, realising her mistake of putting her size fives in it. "Sorry, I didn't think. You'll find the right guy soon enough."

"No need to apologise. As for finding the right soulmate, I don't think swiping left is going to cut it."

Sara laughed. "Ah, that's where you've been going wrong all along, you're supposed to swipe right, not left."

Lorraine rolled her eyes. "See, I'm not cut out for this online dating lark, never have been and, I suspect, never will be in the future." She turned and walked out the front door.

Sara watched her leave, her heart heavy for her friend who was so down in the mouth. Sara suspected her single status was laying heavy on Lorraine's mind more and more lately as the years passed her by. Maybe Sara getting hitched recently had gone a long way in highlighting the issue more in Lorraine's eyes. She shrugged and turned her attention back to walking through the bungalow, searching for clues.

Two white-suited SOCO techs were in the lounge, photographing the open drawers and the mess on the floor. "Tell me to do one if I get in the way, just having a nosy, if you don't mind?"

"Feel free, we're almost done here," one of the men said, clicking away on his camera.

"Anything standing out to you?" Sara rooted around on the floor and examined a few bits of scrap paper with her gloved hand. Nothing to be seen there apart from a few shopping and a couple of to-do lists, in amongst other reminders the old lady had jotted down.

"Her handbag is over there, beside her chair, we've got to bag it up. I had a quick peek and her purse appears to be missing."

"Figures, it wouldn't be a burglary without some money going missing, would it?"

"Yeah, I suppose. In the bedroom, there's a shoebox that's been tampered with; it's lying on the bed, its contents spilled on the quilt."

"I'll go take a look. Sickening, right, chaps?"

Both men agreed with a sharp nod of their hooded heads.

She stepped back into the hallway and went to the back of the house. Sara poked her head into one room. It was a small boxroom with a single bed and a dressing table off to the side. Nothing to see there. No sign of disruption, so she carried on to the room next door.

Shaking her head, she ventured into the room, disgusted that the woman's personal belongings had been rummaged through. *Had this happened before or after she was murdered?*

She crossed the room to the bed and, using her phone, she took a photo of the spilled contents from the box, which contained Val's personal paperwork, including her birth and marriage certificates. Had the burglar been interested in identity fraud, they would have snatched those without a moment's hesitation. It was another significant piece of the puzzle in Sara's eyes.

There was a small bundle of receipts, maybe from the gifts she'd bought for her family at Christmas in case any of them wanted to exchange them for something else. There was also a pretty beaded bracelet which had more than likely been a gift from her granddaughter when she was younger. Lovely to keep as a memento. Other than that, there was very little else left in the box. Sara couldn't help wondering if the woman had kept money in there for any form of emergency, such as paying an extra heating bill in the sharpest of winters.

She glanced around the rest of the room and was drawn to the wardrobe on the far wall. Both doors were wide open and some of Val's clothes were strewn across the floor. She searched the interior, hoping some form of clue would smack her in the face. It didn't. By the look of things, the killer had taken all they needed and left only the victim's clothes behind, having no use for the old woman's taste in fashion.

Sara sighed. *Why? Why kill a defenceless old lady nearing the end of her life? Why not take what you wanted, you bastard, and leave her alive?*

Feeling sick to her stomach and with more questions than answers rattling around in her head, she said farewell to the SOCO techs and left the house. Carla was waiting in the car for her. Sara stripped off her suit and threw it in the black bag by the front door and then climbed in the car beside her partner. "Everything all right?"

"As right as it can be. I thought I'd leave you to it. Couldn't stand going back in the house, knowing that the old lady suffered horribly before she died."

"I get that. On the plus side, her purse is missing. Maybe the perp will slip up and use her bank card in the next few days."

"If she had one. Is it likely, if she kept other funds at her house? Most old people have a distinct lack of trust for banks, in my experience."

Sara started the engine and blew out a frustrated breath. "You could be right. You know what? I detest this killer so much already."

"Me too. Attacking old women in their homes is the lowest of the low in my opinion. Scumbag!"

"I can probably conjure up a few worse names to call them, if I wasn't so tired. I'm going to suggest we call it a day for now. We've both been putting in extra hours lately, the last thing I want to do is screw this case up through tiredness, especially when it involves one of our own."

"I agree. It would have been different if the neighbours had seen anything for us to go on, but they didn't. Right from the word go we're up against it, aren't we?"

"So it would seem."

Sara dropped Carla back to her car at the station and drove home. She entered the house at ten-thirty to find only Misty, the cat, there to greet her. She swept her four-legged friend up into her arms for a cuddle. Misty rubbed her head under Sara's chin and purred loudly. "I bet you're hungry. Let's see what we can find for you."

She reflected on how sad her day had been as she carried Misty into the kitchen and opened the cupboard next to the sink. "Ah-ha, I spy with my little eye a tin of tuna with your name written on it, my little princess." She popped Misty on the floor and opened the tin. After pouring the contents into the cat bowl, she watched contentedly as Misty tucked in.

"Now, I wonder what's on the menu for us." She pulled open the oven door to find it empty and then searched the fridge to find that almost bare. She lifted the egg box, and it was heavy. "Looks like it'll be omelette for dinner then." She withdrew the last of the mushrooms and the remainder of the peppers lying in the fresh drawer. Then she wandered across the room to the veg rack and picked up the last onion. "Someone needs to go shopping, methinks."

She was tempted to ring Mark to see how long he was going to be and possibly hint at picking up a takeaway on his way home, but she chastised herself. "He's got enough on his plate, why bother him? Knuckle down and get on with it, girl."

That's what she did. Disappointed she couldn't make a better meal for the love of her life, she prepared the ingredients to hand. Chopping away all the bad bits on the peppers, she dropped them into the pan, then began frying the contents, adding the final few rashers of bacon as an afterthought. She added the whisked eggs, shook in a few dried herbs and was delighted with the result. A frittata big enough for two. She hoped it would reheat satisfactorily when Mark came in from work; if not, there would be nothing left in the fridge for him to eat and he'd be forced to have beans on toast for dinner.

Sara plated up her meal and took it into the lounge. She sat on the sofa, her legs tucked underneath her and switched on the TV. She changed channels a few times and then settled on a documentary about the effects of climate change. Politicians, especially in the States, had pushed the issue aside for years and now the planet was in severe danger. Her eyelids began to droop; she turned the TV off, finding the programme rather depressing, and washed up her plate.

Misty wound herself around her legs a few times. "Want to go out, Munchkin?"

The cat rushed to the back door, and Sara waited for her to go to the toilet and to return. She glanced up at the stars twinkling in the clear night sky, wishing that Mark was there with her.

After clearing away the dishes she'd used, she wandered upstairs to bed and settled down with the latest Linda S. Prather thriller. It had been a while since the talented author had released a book, so she was eager to dive in. However, she must have been more tired than she realised and found herself struggling to stay awake. Eventually, she placed her Kindle on the bedside table, switched off the light and snuggled down under the quilt. It was eleven-fifteen and still no sign of Mark yet.

A few hours later, Sara's ears pricked up. *Was that the front door?* Whenever Mark worked late, he always had the decency to creep around downstairs so as not to wake her. She strained her ear to listen for his footfalls on the stairs. When he didn't enter the room after a few minutes, that's when the fear struck. *Is it him or is it an intruder?*

Phone in hand, she pulled on her towelling robe and quietly crept down the stairs. She was halfway down when she heard a noise coming from the kitchen.

Swallowing down the bile that had emerged, she tentatively descended the rest of the stairs and pushed open the kitchen door. "My God, it is you. I thought there was a possible stranger in the house. Are you all right?"

Mark slowly turned to face her and she gasped. "Not really."

She rushed towards him and ran a hand over his injured face. His nose was bleeding, his top lip swollen and his right eye was starting to discolour. "Here, sit down. What the hell happened to you, darling?"

"It's nothing. It'll heal. It goes with the territory."

"What? Are you insane? You're a bloody vet, for fuck's sake. What are you talking about? Who did this to you?"

"A client. He brought his German Shepherd in for an examination. Possible hip dysplasia. The examination is often painful for the animal, but I have to see the extent of the disease. The dog cried out, and the guy shouted at me; the next thing I knew, I was lying on my back on the floor after he lumped me one."

"Oh no, my poor baby. Who was it? A regular customer?"

"No, he's new to the area. I took him on, even though the practice is full, and that's the thanks I get."

"Jesus, maybe they handle vets differently where he comes from. Give me his name. He can't be allowed to go around punching people like that, it's assault. We can get him for ABH."

Mark shook his head and waved away her concerns. "No, I understand why he did it. He loves his dog and I hurt her, it shows how much he cares for the animal."

Sara held her husband's damaged face between her hands and kissed him gently on the lips. "And that's why I love you so much. You're such a forgiving, understanding human being."

"I do my best." He laughed and winced.

"Have you been to the hospital?"

"No. It happened a few hours ago, I performed the operation I had planned and then came straight home. I couldn't let the owner of the cat down. I didn't have to see the owner as the cat is staying in to recover overnight, so I wasn't under pressure to get cleaned up."

"You're amazing. Will you let me clean you up?"

"Would you mind? You have a heavy day ahead of you, you should get some sleep."

"I'm awake now. Let me care for my man. Have you eaten?"

He wrapped her in his arms and kissed the top of her head. "No, not yet. Haven't felt hungry until now. What did you have?"

"I've let you down, there wasn't much in the fridge. I knocked up a frittata, yours is in the microwave, not sure how the hell it's going to reheat though. It's there if you want to take a chance."

"You always doubt your cooking abilities and there's no need for you to apologise for not getting the shopping in. We're a partnership, we both work long hours. The onus isn't on you to fill the cupboards, we should both shoulder the blame if they're empty. Got that?"

"I hear you. We should get into a routine of doing it on our days off, but there's always something else to do, isn't there? Anyway, that can keep for another day. Let's see if we have any TCP lying around to clean you up." She kissed him again and then searched the cupboard under the sink. "Bingo. This is likely to sting a little."

He laughed. "It'll be less harmful than the thump I received earlier, so I'm prepared to take a risk."

Sara carefully tended to his wounds. Mark was a brave soldier, only wincing and sucking in a sharp breath a few times during the treatment. Afterwards, she heated up the frittata for him and he demolished it within seconds.

"Someone was hungry. Do you want some ice cream to fill you up?"

"No, that was enough for me. Come on, let's go to bed." He had a twinkle in his eye.

"I'll pour us both a glass of wine, how's that?"

"Sounds good to me."

2

———

*S*ara was the last of the team to arrive the following day. "Sorry, I'm late. Where are we at?"

"Morning," Carla replied, staring at her quizzically.

Sara was keen to get on with the investigation rather than answer her partner's unasked questions. "I need you guys to do some digging, see if there have been any other burglaries in the area in the last six months. I can't recall any ending up in a murder scene, but as we're all aware, criminals escalate over time. Whether out of boredom or something else, I'm not too sure. Let's get armed with the facts and go from there."

Roger Purcell walked into the incident room. "Hello, ma'am. Sorry to interrupt. Would it be okay if we had a chat?"

"Of course, Roger. Come into my office."

The team muttered as they left the room. Sara motioned for him to go into the office ahead of her. "Can I get you a coffee?"

"Please, white with one sugar."

"Carla, sorry, do you mind bringing us two white coffees with one, please?"

Carla nodded and shot out of her chair. Sara entered the office and left the door ajar. She removed her coat, hung it on the rack and then sat behind her desk opposite Roger. "Let's get the daft question out of the way first. How are you today?"

"Confused would be my answer, I suppose."

Sara noted the suit he was wearing and said, "I can understand that. You're not back at work yet, are you?"

"Yes, I'd be hopeless at home." He held up a hand. "I swear I'm not here to hound you about the investigation."

Sara smiled. "Glad to hear it, you know these things take time to get going."

"I know. I wanted to touch base with you. Tell you what my daughter said about her visit yesterday."

Sara sat back and steepled her fingers. Carla pushed open the door, placed two cups on the table and left the room again, closing the door behind her. "Go on."

"Sonia called in to see Mum after college. She told me Mum was in good spirits when she left. Was about to put her feet up and watch some TV. Sonia's distraught by what has happened to her grandmother. I sense she's going to be blaming herself for years to come."

"Why should she blame herself?" Sara sat forward and took a sip from her cup.

"My lass is a sensitive soul. She believes if she'd stayed a little while longer, then her grandmother would still be alive today."

Sara sighed. "No one can know that for sure. For all we know, the killer might have been watching the house, waiting to seize the opportunity to strike."

"That's what I told her, sort of. Any news from the neighbours? Sorry, forgive me, I shouldn't be asking you that, this is your investigation, not mine."

"I get where you're coming from. It's going to be hard for you to let go and allow us to proceed, but you're going to have to do it; otherwise, it'll eat away at you. I promise you we're going to go the extra mile on this one. Not just because the victim was your mother, but because I detest any kind of assault or crime against the frailer members of our community."

"I appreciate your point of view. Most officers would put a case like this on the back burner from the outset."

Sara inclined her head. "Not me, I can assure you. I have a few questions for you if you're up to answering them?"

He reached for his cup, took a swig and then nodded. "Fire away."

Sara studied his ageing face. She took him to be in his mid-to-late forties. His hair showing signs of age at the sides. His face gaining a few wrinkles here and there. "Did your mother have any money at the house?"

"Yes, don't tell me the bastard got to it?" He fidgeted in his seat and then lifted his cup again.

"It would appear that way. There was a box lying on the bed with all her personal paperwork left in it."

"Yes, she used to keep some money there. Although, saying that, I think she had it dotted around in several places. And before you say it, I warned her about the dangers of keeping cash in the house, but she wouldn't listen. Hard to argue with her views about not trusting banks when they're currently screwing us over with pathetic interest rates."

"I wholeheartedly agree with you. Did your mother still use a bank, to pay any direct debits, for instance?"

"Yes, she's with Lloyds. Why?"

After taking a drink of coffee, Sara said, "We found her handbag, but her purse was missing."

He shook his head slowly and his expression darkened. "I can't believe what I'm hearing. I still can't get my head around why anyone would kill a pensioner in their own home."

"I know. It doesn't sit well with me either. I'll put a stop to her card at the bank."

"Why? There isn't much in there. I'm giving you permission to leave the account open. That way you can track the bastard down if they decide to use it." He raked a hand through his hair, mussing it up. "She kept her damn pin number written on a piece of paper beside her card."

"Shit. Okay, let's think of it as a positive and see if we can trap the bugger. I'll get on to the bank, set up an alert for them to contact us if the card is used, how's that?"

"Sounds like an exceptional plan to me. If I ever get my hands on that no-mark..."

"I understand how you feel, but please, let's catch the bastard first and let the courts decide what happens to them."

"Ha, that's a laugh. I did a study on court cases a few years ago, started with the immediate area and then widened the search to national, and the results were mind-numbing. Without saying it, the number of judges who give a lesser sentence for crimes against the elderly is disgusting. I wasn't aware until a colleague pointed it out to me with a case she was working on. She was right, too. What is it with our bloody society? She did a study herself and found that crimes against youngsters and the elderly are treated poorly in the eyes of the law."

"That's appalling to hear. I've never really studied the statistics before, not in depth anyway. All I can do is my best, heap the evidence on the culprit, if that's what it takes to get a heavier sentence for them."

"If it works. I have my doubts, after seeing the facts myself. Sorry, I'm veering off track here. I think it's important that my colleagues should know about this, though, don't you?"

Sara studied the skyline outside the window for a moment and then said thoughtfully, "Absolutely. I suppose it's within our grasp to try and change things."

"We bust a gut to get the fuckers, excuse my language, to court and then the judges seem to do the dirty on us. Maybe someone should start a petition and present it to the House of Lords. Perhaps the powers that be might think twice about the sentences they hand down in the future."

"I'd sign up for that, if you want to action something. Always willing to help a colleague when it comes to making changes to the justice system."

"Deal. Sorry to go off course. Is there anything else you wanted to ask me?"

"Not really, except to say that once SOCO have finished at the house, it might be worth you searching for your mother's hiding places and see what you can find."

"I'll do that. I know a few of them, I doubt if she would tell me where they all were, knowing Mum. No doubt we'll come across some extra ones when it comes to stripping out the house and putting it up for sale."

"I don't envy you that task."

"Thanks. My wife will help me out there, she's great at organising things like that."

"That's a blessing. Dividing up a deceased's estate can be traumatic at the best of times. Do you and your sister get on?" Sara reflected how difficult it had been for her parents to cope with when her grandparents had died.

"Thankfully, yes. We've always been supportive of each other. My wife had problems with her family when her own mother died. Getting back to Mum, do you think that's why the intruder killed her? You know, because she refused to tell him or her where she'd stashed the cash?"

"Possibly. I suppose we'll never really find that out unless the culprit is caught and decides to spill the beans."

He finished his coffee and nodded. "Anything else I can help you with?"

"I think that's all. I know I've said it before, but I want to reaffirm that you have my word; we'll do our very best to find your mother's killer."

"After coming here today, I have no doubt about it. Thank you, Inspector Ramsey."

She wagged a finger. "It's Sara. Thanks for coming in. Take care of yourself. If grief descends, promise me you'll call it a day and go home."

"I promise."

He left the room. Sara stared out of the window, lost in thought as she finished her own drink. Then she left the office and brought the team up to date with what Roger had told her. "So, let's crack on with things. I want this one wrapped up ASAP, can't bear the thought of other pensioners being targeted by this person, presuming they're not going to stop at just one murder, especially if it turned out to be profitable in the process." Sara shuddered. "Why are some human beings so vile? It's beyond me at times. The last case we dealt with in this vein turned out to be about fuelling the individual's drug habit, let's hope this one isn't the same."

"That was a particularly bad case, I seem to remember," Carla added.

"One of the worst I've dealt with during my career. Saying that, none of them are 'good cases', are they?"

Carla rolled her eyes and nodded.

"Okay, so, Jill and Marissa, I want you guys to search the database, broaden the search you did earlier, see if there have been any attempted burglaries on *pensioners* in the area in the past six months. I wouldn't bother looking for murders because I think if there had been, we would have been involved in the case."

"Okay," Jill replied, giving Marissa the thumbs-up. Marissa remained seated until the meeting was finished.

"Craig and Barry, why don't you get busy with the CCTV footage, if there is any in the area?"

"Is it going to be worth it, boss? I mean, with no vehicle details to hand."

Sara sighed. "You've got me on that one. Maybe source the footage anyway, just in case something comes to light during the day. Perhaps one of the neighbours might recall seeing a car during the morning or something." She raised her crossed fingers. "You never know. I'm going to get on to the bank. Roger has agreed to keep his mother's account active in the hope the perp will use her card. I need to pre-warn the bank and ask them to get in touch with us as soon as her card is used. That is, if the killer decides to use it, which is a distinct possibility if their main aim was to extract cash from the victim in the first place. I also need to ring SOCO, see if they can turn the place upside down for us to try and find any extra cash the victim might have been hiding. I'd hate for the perp to return and find it before we've had the chance to locate it."

"Is that likely?" Carla asked, frowning.

Sara shrugged. "Your guess is as good as mine."

"I'll ring SOCO, if you want?" Carla suggested.

"Thanks, saves me a job. Right, let's get things started, peeps." She left the incident room and entered her office via the vending machine. It usually took two cups of coffee to get her going in the morning. When she called the bank manager, he turned out to be very accommodating. Mr Osbourne stated that he would ensure all the cameras on the ATMs were working correctly and would send over any subsequent footage that came his way regarding the use of the victim's card. Sara thanked him and ended the call.

Then she picked up the phone and rang Mark.

"Hey you. I was just thinking about you."

"You were? Saucy thoughts at work, you naughty man." Hearing Mark's easy-going tone boosted her mood.

Mark laughed. "Hardly. I was going to ring you to suggest meeting up and going to the supermarket after work, so we can do a weekly shop together. What say you?"

"Hmm… that's a tad disappointing but practical, I suppose. It would have been nicer if you'd said I'll meet you in town and we'll go out for a nice meal together. But hey-ho!"

"There's nothing stopping us from doing that after we've finished the shopping. I hear Morrison's café run special offers on their meals during the week."

"What the…?"

Mark laughed. "I can just imagine the downright disgust on your face at this moment. I was pulling your leg. I wouldn't do that to you."

"Phew, glad to hear it. If we're watching the pennies, we could go to the Cock at Tupsley, they have a two-for-one offer on."

"Sounds good. It's just up the road from Morrison's too. What time shall I meet you?"

"Meet me at the supermarket at six-fifteen, is that okay?"

"Perfect. I've got no extra surgeries planned this evening, so there's no reason why I shouldn't be there on time."

"Good. How's the nose by the way? That's the reason I was calling you."

"It's fine, a little sore, but nothing too bad. Thanks for caring."

"Of course I care. Nevertheless, I still reckon you should lay assault charges on the thug who attacked you."

"Not going to happen, love, so it's a waste of time you trying to twist my arm."

"Worth a try. He needs to be taught a lesson in self-control, if nothing else. I'm sure a night in the cells would sort him out."

"Sara," he warned.

She groaned inwardly, all she wanted to do was support him, the way he always supported her. "All right. I'll back off. Think about it though, I'd willingly drop round to his place and read him the riot act on your behalf. What's the use of being married to an inspector if I can't intercept now and again?"

"Ha bloody ha, no way, Sara. There's no point, the bloke was concerned about his dog. To me, that's a positive in this world, not a negative; there are plenty of people out there who don't give a stuff about their animals. Let's leave this here, okay?"

"I suppose. Okay, you've won this round."

"The final round."

"All right. End of subject, I'll see you around six-fifteen, unless anything major strikes beforehand."

"You're on. Have a good day and thanks for calling."

"You too. Try to dodge any flying fists, if you can," she chuckled.

"I've learnt my lesson, don't worry."

Sara ended the call and grabbed a handful of paperwork to get started on.

3

$\mathcal{H}$e watched and waited for someone to enter the alley. His heart pounding as the adrenaline rushed through his veins. This was all the high he needed to get his fix while some people relied on drugs to make them feel this way. He had other means of obtaining his pleasures. Five minutes quickly turned into ten, his leg bounced and he drummed his fingers on the steering wheel to help keep him occupied.

A young blonde woman, tottering on four-inch heels, entered the alley. He liked what he saw, he preferred petite women he could easily control. His dick sprang into action and throbbed against his zip.

Jumping out of the car, he followed the young woman down the alley. Halfway down, he made his move. His hand slapped over her mouth, rendering her powerless to scream. She lashed out with her arms, but didn't manage to make contact.

"You're going to be mine. Fight it and I'll kill you, you got that?"

He swivelled the girl to look at him and adjusted his hold over her mouth. Her eyes doubled in size. She shook her head and his hand suppressed her muffled pleas. Her gaze flitted to either end of the alley, but it was pointless; he knew very few people used this as a shortcut nowadays. It had taken around ten minutes for her to appear while he was waiting.

"You and I are going to have some fun." He raised a knee, pinning her in place against the wooden fence and reached into his pocket. He extracted a length of rope and a pair of black socks. He was already wearing gloves.

She tried to wriggle out of his grasp. His knee dug into her stomach, causing her to wince. She stared at him, her eyes welling up with tears of frustration.

"What did I tell you? Fight the inevitable and I'll kill you."

"Please, don't hurt me." He could just make out her muffled plea.

"Be good and I won't." He shoved the socks in her mouth. She gagged several times. Then he tied her arms behind her back and forced her to the ground. She tried to resist, but with her arms now restricted, he found it easy to gain access to her panties.

"No, no, not that, please." Her muffled response was clear enough for him to understand.

He stared at her and grinned. "Yes, please. I want what you have to offer. You girls think it's all right to wear short skirts and high heels. You do that and this is what's going to happen."

She shook her head and then turned to the side and squeezed her eyes shut as he ripped off her panties. Her thrashing ceased, accepting what was about to happen.

Once the deed was done, he roughly grabbed her chin and forced her to face him. "How was it for you?"

Tears flowing, she gagged numerous times on the pair of socks. Fear reached her eyes. He laughed and watched her suffering, not caring if she lived or died.

The choking continued and the panic rose in her eyes.

His hand latched around her throat and he throttled her until she lay still, her eyes permanently wide open now. Dead.

He stood, pulled the zip up on his trousers and trotted up the alley to his car. He felt numb, no feelings either way. But as he drove away, the euphoria erupted and he laughed until tears seeped from his eyes. He drove home, but stopped off at the off-licence to pick up a four-pack of lagers, which he had every intention of downing the minute he stepped through the front door.

An idea sparked when he got out of the car and saw the ATM on the wall outside the small Tesco's. He adjusted his cap and put the old woman's card in the slot, then dug around in his pocket for the slip of paper he'd found in her purse on which she'd written the pin number. He punched the number in and selected the 'other amount' button on the screen, then manually added three hundred pounds as a withdrawal figure.

He glanced around him, making sure there wasn't anyone else close enough to see him, or worse still, to try and rob him once the cash came out.

After collecting the notes, he went into Oddbins and picked up a pack of Fosters, paid for them and returned to the car.

He smiled at how easy it was to get the money from the woman's account. *Another three hundred again tomorrow and the next day, and I'll be laughing for a few weeks.*

4

*E*n route to the crime scene and after postponing the shopping trip and dinner date with Mark, Sara let out an expressive sigh. "Jesus, as if we haven't got enough to deal with at the moment. Why is it we always get lumbered with having to run two cases at the same time?"

Carla kept quiet, she knew better than to say anything to the contrary when Sara was letting rip.

"Say something," Sara shouted.

"Maybe, when you've calmed down, I'll be able to get a word in."

"Sorry, I'm terrible when I get going."

"We need to blame it on the cutbacks. Every team at the station is under pressure, right?"

"Yeah. But bitching about it makes me feel a whole lot better." *If only you knew! I still have no idea who I need to set free on the team, and I've got to make that decision within the next month. Oh, joy of joys!*

Carla sniggered. "Which is why I let you rant away."

"Sometimes you're wiser than you let on, aren't you?"

"I have my moments, especially where your moods are concerned."

"Charming! I wasn't aware that I had mood swings."

"Let's just say they've been getting worse over the past few weeks."

"They have? Why didn't you tell me?"

Carla faced her and grinned. "I value my job."

"Bloody cheek. You know you're allowed to speak freely around me, especially when we're alone."

"I know, but you saying it, and me acting upon it, are two different things entirely."

Sara tutted and pulled up alongside the SOCO vans at the end of the alley. "Lucky our journey has come to an end. We'll continue this conversation later. Let's suit up before Lorraine has a hissing fit."

"Wonder how she is today."

"I was just thinking the same. I bet she hasn't had a chance to perform the PM on yesterday's victim yet, and now she's got another one to deal with."

"She'll come good, she always does."

"I'm still going to tread carefully around her today."

They left the car and stepped into their paper suits, then went in search of Lorraine. They found her instructing the SOCO technicians a few feet from the body.

Sara stared down at the victim. She shook her head. The girl couldn't have been much more than twenty-five. *Her whole life ahead of her and now, she's dead!*

"Shocking, isn't it? To die so young. And yes, I believe she was raped."

"Any DNA left on her?"

"Nope, none found so far."

"What was the time of death, any idea?"

"Around two hours ago, max. I rang you as soon as I was notified."

"Oh, so you're the one to blame for handing us another case so soon after starting the other one."

"Sorry, I figured as long as I was under the cosh, you might as well join me. Sharing is caring and all that."

Sara sighed. "Thanks. If only you knew the pressure we're under right now."

"Aren't we all? I haven't even touched yesterday's victim yet, and no, I'm not guilty of postponing it. If you must know, I had a road traffic accident victim to attend to around midnight."

"Crap, I thought you looked tired. I steered clear of mentioning it because of how upset you were yesterday."

"I'm over that. I gave myself a good talking to just before I attended the accident. I came into work this morning prepared to go ahead with the PM on the old lady when the phone rang and I got diverted to attend this one. Another heart-breaker, but then, aren't they all?"

"Yep. Young or old, they're all the same to me. Neither of them should have been killed, in my opinion." She glanced up and down the alley, shuddering as the breeze whistled through the gap and then stated, "The killer knew exactly what he was doing. I bet this place isn't used that often."

"According to the fella who popped his head over the fence, only a handful of people use the alley now the new pedestrian bridge down the road has been put in."

She stared down at the victim. "Which begs the question, why did she use it? Where was she going? Do you have an ID for her?"

"In the evidence bag over there. Maybe she was on her way to work."

Sara raised an eyebrow. "Dressed like that in the middle of the day?"

"I'm surmising, don't shoot me down in flames like that."

"That wasn't my intention, sorry. Maybe she's a sex-worker and this is where she hangs out."

Carla laughed. "I don't think she'd get much passing trade, boss."

Sara cringed at her dumb suggestion. "All right, smart arse."

"In all seriousness, Carla is right. She wouldn't get any passing trade down here," Lorraine chipped in.

"All right. You've both missed what I was getting at completely. She would need to take her tricks somewhere to do the deed, right?"

Carla nodded and Lorraine rolled her eyes. "You're not as silly as you look," Lorraine added.

"Thanks. I'll take that as a compliment. Of course, until we speak to a family member, all this is speculation. I might be doing her an injustice. Maybe she was going on a date. Or to a job interview."

"Dressed like that? Carla asked. "What type of job?"

"All right, this isn't getting us anywhere. Carla, jot down her name and address if you can find it and we'll ask the necessary questions once we've tracked down her family."

Carla went in search of the evidence bag and wrote down the details needed, then returned to stand beside Sara. "She lives a few roads over that way."

"Okay, yet another depressing couple of hours ahead of us then. What am I saying? It's part of the job, right?"

"Unfortunately, we all have our crosses to bear. I'd willingly swap duties for the next few hours, if you're up for it?" Lorraine smiled sarcastically.

"Er... no thanks. Not going to happen. I'll stop whining and accept our fate. Anything else for us before we go on our way? Cause of death maybe?"

"Petechial haemorrhaging is telling me she was strangled."

"So she was raped and then strangled. How horrendous, she must have gone through a terrible ordeal. Fucking bastard. If we ever catch up with him, I'll be tempted to cut his dick off."

Lorraine laughed. "I can see that going down well at Head Office."

"Yeah, my head would be on the platter soon after, I suspect. Okay, we're going to get off then and leave you to it. Will you be shifting her soon?" Sara pointed at the small crowd gathering at the bottom of the alley.

"Yeah, I'm not going to put a tent up; they're far enough away not to matter. I will cover her face in a second or two while I finish up and make the arrangements to get her moved."

"Very wise. Well, let me know how the PMs go when you get a spare second, if you would?"

"I will. Good luck with tracing a relative."

"Thanks. Speak soon." Sara turned on her heel and, with Carla beside her, they both marched back to the car. "Do I need to put the address in the satnav?"

"Nope, I'll give you directions."

Carla was right, the woman's flat was a few streets away, not far from the alley where she'd lost her life.

"I hate to think that she was within bloody spitting distance of safety. It reeks of someone stalking her, acquainted with where she lived and perhaps which route she took, or is that my overactive imagination at work there?"

"You might be right, hard to tell without knowing more about the victim. Maybe she had an ex who refused to take no for an answer."

"An if-I-can't-have-you-nobody-can-have-you scenario," Sara replied, contemplatively.

Carla hitched up her right shoulder. "Why not? It's not as if we have anything else to go on at present."

"There is that. Okay, let's knock on the door, see if anyone else lives here with her. I have a gut feeling she lived alone."

Carla cocked an eyebrow. "I'm never one to doubt your gut feelings, but how in the world would you even know that?"

Sara grinned. "I wouldn't take that as read until we know the answer." She rang the doorbell to the ground floor flat. There was no reply. Sara decided to ring the bell to the flat above. A young woman with blonde hair tied back in a ponytail answered the door.

"Can I help you?"

Sara flashed her warrant card. "We're trying to contact Mona, but she's not home. Can you tell us if anyone else lives here with her?"

"No. There was a chap who used to hang around up until a few months ago, but I haven't seen or heard him, if you get what I mean, not for months."

"Are you insinuating they used to row a lot?"

"When they weren't having noisy sex sessions, yes."

"Oh, I get you. Do you happen to know his name?"

"Jack something. Can't give you more than that, sorry. Is there something wrong?" Her brow wrinkled.

"We can't say. How well do you know Mona?"

"Well enough. Why? What's she done wrong?"

"Nothing as far as we know. Does she have any family members nearby?"

"Yeah, I think her father is around here somewhere. She did tell me, but I've forgotten. She's been in contact with him more recently than she ever did before because there was some kind of bereavement in the family. She did tell me, but I switched off, can't be doing with maudlin stuff like that. I'm one of these people who believe in positivity being the key for a peaceful life. As soon as anyone starts getting a downer, I'm out of there."

"What if that person was crying out for help? Would you still be willing to turn your back on them?"

The young woman bit down on her lip. "Well, when you put it like that, I suppose I did come across as a bit of a bitch."

"Just pointing out the obvious," Sara said. "Please, it'd be a great help if you could try to remember where Mona's father lives."

"Why? What's it to you? Hang on, why ask for her father...? Oh, God! Has something happened to Mona? Is that what you're getting at?"

Sara sighed. "Yes, I can't lie. We need to get in touch with a member of her family desperately."

"How desperately? I can tell something is wrong now, is it serious? Don't tell me that fucker did something to her?"

"Her father?"

She tutted in annoyance. "No, not him. The ex, Jack. I saw him hanging around here for a few weeks after they split up. Heard her shout across the road at him one day, told him to piss off. When he refused to take the hint, she asked one of the blokes from work to accompany her home and pretend he was her boyfriend. He stayed overnight and well, Jack must have taken the hint because he hasn't shown his face around here since."

"I see. Where does she work?"

"She works at a bar in town. The Scrawny Owl, I think it's called." She laughed. "No, it's not, it's the Tawny Owl, I'm such a div at times."

"Does she work full- or part-time?"

"It was a full-time position, although her hours have been cut recently due to the pandemic and the lasting effects on the licensing trade. A lot of the staff got laid off, she's damn lucky they only cut her hours. I think the boss likes her though, more than the other girls on the staff, if you get my drift?"

"I do. Thanks for all your help. Any joy with remembering her father's address? Sorry to push you, it's really important."

"Yeah, you said that before. Go on, tell me what's happened to her, I need to know if I'm safe here or not."

"Why would you believe you weren't safe?"

"I've just told you about the trouble she had with Jack, haven't I? Weren't you listening to me?"

"Of course. You also mentioned that he hadn't been around for a while."

"I get the feeling you're making this difficult, can I ask why? You're avoiding something, I can tell."

"I'm not. I'm simply eager to find Mona's father. If you don't know where he lives, how about you giving me his name or possibly where he works?"

The young woman fell silent for a few moments and banged her backside against the wall as she thought. "Don't quote me on this, but I think he works in a sports shop in town, or he used to."

"Can you think of the name or where it's situated?"

"In the centre of town, near Debenhams, at least I think it is."

"Fantastic. I'm going to leave you a card. If you should think of anything else, please ring me."

"I will. What about Mona, are you going to tell me where she is or what's wrong with her?"

Sara smiled at the woman. "Not right now."

"Wow, that's reassuring, thanks for that."

Sara and Carla left and felt the force of the door slamming behind them. "Jesus, how could I tell her Mona was dead? I sensed she would have had a meltdown there and then, I didn't want to deal with that."

"You did the right thing. We need to tell the family first."

"There is no easy way of dealing with an investigation in this life, is there?"

"It must feel like that at times, but you did okay. Don't ever doubt your capabilities, Sara."

She shook off the cloud of uncertainty and smiled at Carla. "Thanks, I needed that. Back to it. A sports shop near Debenhams, can you think of any?"

"Nope, not right now."

She laughed. "I hope I don't feel guilty stepping inside. I haven't exercised in ages. I used to run a lot, but that appears to have been knocked on the head since I've tied the knot." She glanced down and pulled up her jumper to show a slight overhang to her trousers. "Damn, that sight has just put a downer on my day. Maybe we should both join a gym and go after work, what do you say?"

"As it happens, I've just started going. We could make it a regular thing, but then, you're newlywed and eager to get back to hubby at the end of your shift, unlike me."

"We'll see." They got back in the car and Sara drove into town. She parked in Tesco's underground car park and had a word with the girl at the kiosk counter. She flashed her ID. "We're on important police business. I've parked in the car park, I hope that's okay?"

"It is. Just come and see me when you're ready to go and I'll waive the parking fee for you."

"That'd be super. See you soon."

They swept out of the main entrance and walked the length of the car park, which was heaving with cars, and crossed the main road. "There it is."

She pushed open the main door to the small shop. There were two male customers searching through the rails of leisure wear and a male and a female dealing with what appeared to be a new delivery of stock at the till area. They approached and the male glanced up.

"Hello, there, can we help at all?"

Sara showed him her warrant card. "We're looking for a Mr Load."

He frowned and straightened to his full height, which meant he was towering over Sara. "That would be me. Police? Is there something wrong? I haven't done anything I shouldn't have done, not as far as I know."

"It would be better if we spoke alone, sir. Is there a room out the back we can use?"

"Now you're worrying me. Okay, Abby, mind the shop for me. Give me a shout if you're unsure about anything."

"Oh my, what about using the till?" The young woman seemed terrified at the prospect.

"It's okay. Just give me a call if a customer wants to buy something."

The girl nodded, her gaze flitting between the customers and her boss.

Mr Load led them through a narrow passageway to a tiny office near the back of the property. "This place is a dive, sorry, we tend to spend most of our time out the front. Sorry about Abby, she's new, I'll have to go if she needs me, I haven't started training her on the till yet." He laughed. "That should be fun. She's the type who is scared of her own shadow, that one." He shook his head. "It was a different story entirely when she came for the job last month, she was brimming with confidence which is why I took her on."

Sara smiled. "I'm sure she'll come good under your expert guidance, Mr Load."

"Yes, yes. I hope you're right. Perhaps you wouldn't mind telling me why you're here."

Sara prepared to destroy this man's world. Her breathing became ragged, she inhaled a steady breath and motioned for him to sit down in the one chair in the room. "Take a seat."

He fell into it, his gaze fixed on her concerned face. "What is it?"

"Sir, it's with regret I have to tell you that we believe your daughter's body was found earlier today."

His hand touched the side of his face and his brow furrowed. "I don't understand. Her body? Mona's? What are you saying? That she's dead?" His hand trembled, and he thrust it into his lap.

"I'm sorry. Yes. There's really no easy way of telling you. I'm so sorry for your loss."

"Are you?" he snapped. "Why? You don't know me from bloody Adam. Why should you feel sorry for me?"

Sara was taken aback by the venom in his words. His mood had switched from congenial to angry in a flash. While the man's reaction was understandable, it still came as a shock. She stared at him, lost for words for a moment.

Carla saw her struggling and stepped in. "We appreciate how upset you must be, Mr Load, please, breaking the news to you isn't any easier than you receiving it, I can assure you." Carla's stern tone appeared to break through his rage.

"No, it's me who should be apologising. It was just a shock to hear that my baby girl is dead." His head dipped and his hands covered his face. He openly sobbed in front of them.

Sara and Carla glanced at each other, unsure about how to proceed. In the end, Sara decided it would be best to let him cry, to try to heal his inner emotions.

Eventually, Mr Load dropped his hands and wiped his tears on the cuff of his blue woollen jumper. He stared at Sara and said one word, "How?"

She hesitated for a moment and then said, "I'm sorry, she was murdered." She decided to keep the fact that his daughter had been raped out of the equation for now, at least. Fearing the news would only compound how upset he was.

His head shook slowly. "Why? I can't believe she's gone. We only lost her mother last year and now... my baby is with her. Why? How could this be happening? What have we done to deserve such misery? Hasn't the world seen enough death and destruction over the past year or so? Why would someone knowingly choose to take another person's life when we've all spent the past year trying to save each other's? It makes no bloody sense to me at all."

"I know, it's so hard for us to fathom at this time. Are you up to answering some questions for us?"

"Not really, but if you're saying it'll help your investigation, then yes, ask your damn questions." He inhaled a breath. "I'm sorry, I didn't mean to snap. I'm shocked to the core and have no control over the anger bubbling inside me at this moment."

"Honestly, we have broad shoulders. You don't need to apologise, we understand completely how raw your emotions must be at present. Can you tell us when you last saw your daughter?"

"Yesterday. She came to dinner last night. We spent the evening going through the family photo albums and reminiscing about her mother. Jesus, that sounds so profound. Do you think it was a sign? It was her decision to look through the photos."

"Did she give you a reason?"

"No."

"What sort of mood was she in?"

"She was her usual bubbly self to begin with, but once we opened the albums, we both became reflective and quiet. We were a very close-knit family. Although she moved out to set up house on her own years ago, she knew she could return any day and she did, stay over I mean, frequently."

"What about last night?"

"No. She went home last night. Don't tell me this wouldn't have happened to her if she'd stayed with me last night. I couldn't bear the thought of knowing that, if it were true."

"I don't think so. According to the pathologist, your daughter died a few hours ago. Do you have any idea where she was going?"

He sighed and stared at Sara, his expression pained and full of emotion. "I'm not sure. Where did you find her?"

"In an alley, close to her house. It would appear she was taking a shortcut, at least that's our perception at this stage."

"God! Not that damn alley, I warned her about going down there by herself, especially at night, but you say this occurred today? In broad daylight and nobody saw it?"

"We've yet to canvass the area. We've got uniformed police doing that right now. Our main priority was to track you down and break the news to you before you possibly heard it on the TV or radio."

"Thank you, I appreciate that more than you know. It's important for loved ones to hear as soon as it happens. I can't think of anything worse than hearing about something so tragic through the media. Do you have a suspect in custody?"

"Not yet. There was no one at the crime scene."

"I know, it was a dumb question, one I had to ask." He shook his head. "I don't know what else to say, my mind is full of nonsensical questions that I'm too scared to ask. The truth is I don't want to know the ins and outs of how she died, however, I'm aware that I should know. Does that make sense? Because it doesn't to me, none of this does. I'm appalled to be in this position less than twelve months since her mother passed away. How the hell can I bury my daughter? I've never bargained on having to do this throughout my life, you just don't, do you?"

"I feel for you, it's not something we tend to make plans for, saying goodbye to someone so young." Sara's voice cracked and she coughed to clear her throat as images of her dying Philip pushed into her mind.

Carla placed a hand on her arm and mouthed, "Are you all right?"

"Am I missing something here?" Mr Load asked, watching the interaction between Sara and Carla.

It was Carla who spoke first. "The inspector's husband was murdered a few years ago."

He stared at Sara open-mouthed for a brief second and then whispered, "So, you truly do know what I'm going through."

"I do. And I have to say you're going to have some dark times ahead of you, believe me."

He smiled. "I'll have to dig deep and drag up the happy times from my memory bank to keep me on the straight and narrow then, won't I?"

"You will. Perhaps you can tell us if Mona had mentioned being under stress lately for any reason?"

"I don't think so. Not that she let on. Stress as in a bad day at work? How would that lead to her death, Inspector?"

"It wouldn't, I meant stress as in her personal life."

"No, nothing is coming to mind. You're not hinting at someone who she knew doing this to her, are you?"

"Possibly. Okay, here's the deal. We called at Mona's flat and spoke to the young woman above. She told us that Mona had split up with her boyfriend a few months ago. What can you tell us about either him or their relationship?"

"Nothing much. I never really got on with Jack. To me, it appeared he lacked any sense of compassion, you know, regarding what Mona had been through the past year, trying to overcome the loss of her mother on top of the damn pandemic and everything that involved. It was a shitty time for each and every one of us. Thankfully, we didn't lose anyone due to the virus, unlike a couple of friends of ours."

"That's terrible. So many lives were lost during that time. How often did Mona see Jack?"

"Quite often. They were very close, I can't say she loved him, though, otherwise she wouldn't have split up with him, would she? I think he stayed at her flat a few nights during the week, but she was keen to keep hold of her freedom and refused to let him move in when he raised the subject, cheeky sod. I was extremely proud of her standing her ground. Shit! I get where this is leading, do you think he did this? Did he kill my baby?"

Sara raised her hand. "That's impossible to know at this stage. He'll definitely be a person of interest. I don't suppose you happen to know where we can find him? What his surname is or where he works, perhaps?"

He thought over the questions for a few moments. "Surname, I haven't got a clue. I think she said he's a porter at the hospital, or did she? Something is prodding me to think that, I'm sorry, I'm not being much help, am I?"

"You're doing fine. Carla, can you ring the hospital for me?"

Carla nodded and left the room.

Mr Load blew out a large breath that puffed out his rosy cheeks. "I feel so claustrophobic in here. I hate this area, we spend most of the time either on the shop floor or in the stockroom next door. I avoid this place like the plague usually."

"Do you want to move? I don't mind, it's up to you."

"Are you going to be long now?"

"I don't think so."

"Let's get it over with quickly then, Abby will probably interrupt us soon anyway, sod's law, right?"

"It's bound to happen," Sara agreed. "Can you think of anyone Mona had fallen out with lately?"

"She wasn't the type. She tended to brush people aside if they argued with her. My girl liked to live a simple life, no conflicts if she could help it."

"What about Jack? How did that end?"

"Let me think?" He paused for a while and then clicked his fingers. "I believe he started hounding her about moving into her place because his landlord was evicting him. I seem to recall the bloke had sold the house where Jack was staying. He was cheesed off, too lazy to search for other accommodation and plonked himself on Mona's sofa and refused to move."

"How did she eventually get rid of him?"

"She tricked him. Gave him a tenner to go and fetch some beers and locked him out of the house. She was wise enough not to give him a key to the front door."

Sara smiled. "She sounds as though she had her head screwed on."

Tears welled up. "She did. I'm going to miss her terribly. She was my only child and now, with my wife gone as well, I'm left all alone. I'm not sure how I'm going to cope. She was my shoulder to cry on when things got on top of me. This is my business, things have been rough the past year as you can imagine. I was forced to take out a large loan to restock the shop and I'm a long way off recouping that money. It's so stressful being self-employed during these worrying times."

"I'm sure it is. Maybe you can get in touch with a counselling service."

He grunted. "Not for me. The last thing I want or need right now is to be baring my soul to a complete stranger."

"Honestly, sometimes speaking to an outsider, someone who doesn't know you, can truly make a difference to what goes on up here," she said, pointing at her temple.

"Did you do it? When you lost your husband?"

"I had to. I would have gone crazy if I hadn't. Take my word for it, unburdening yourself rather than dwelling on things is a great healer. You should consider it in the near future."

His head lowered and he mumbled. "I'll think about it. I'm sorry you had to deal with such a loss at your young age, that can't have been easy. Did it affect your career?"

"It wasn't easy. What doesn't break us makes us stronger, so they say; I happen to believe that's true. Yes, it affected my career, but not in the way you might think. I moved areas, I used to live in Liverpool. I came back to Hereford to be with my family."

"Wow, that must have taken some guts, coping with such an upheaval while you were going through the grieving process."

"I got on with it. Slotting into a new team usually has its own challenges, but the guys here all took to me straight away and we've had a lot of success as a team since then. I want to assure you, we won't rest until we find whoever did this to your daughter."

"Thank you, I needed to hear you say that. Are you over the loss of your husband now? How long has it been since he...?"

"Three years. I must admit, I think of him often, especially at times such as this when I have to share bad news with a victim's family."

"I can imagine. My wife died eleven months ago and it's still very raw."

Sara placed a hand over his. "Which is why I suggested you seek help. The experts will guide you through these dark times, I promise you."

"Thanks for the chat, tell me, have you since found happiness?"

Sara held up her left hand. "Yes, I've met a wonderful man and we got married a few months ago."

He smiled. "That's wonderful. Maybe I'll meet someone else in the near future."

"Someone will walk into your life when you're least expecting it, I promise. It's what happened to me. I met Mark, who is a vet, when my cat got poisoned. He saved her life and stole my heart the same day."

With his smile still prominent, he said, "You're lucky to have found love a second time around. I doubt if I will because I still think about my wife each waking moment and now my time is going to be spent reflecting on whether if I could have done more for my daughter." His chin dipped to his chest.

"You didn't let her down, you can't punish yourself by thinking that way."

"Easier to say than do, I suspect."

Carla returned to the room. "I have what we need."

"Good. We'll shoot over there and have a word with him now. That is, if you're going to be okay, Mr Load. Or do you want us to stick around for a little while longer? Perhaps you have some questions you want us to answer."

"No, I want you to get out there and find my daughter's killer. Any questions I may have can wait. I'm sure I'll think of a hundred or more when you leave."

"Here's my card, don't hesitate to get in touch."

He took the card from her and stood. He looked Sara in the eye and whispered, "Thank you for sparing the time to have a little chat with me. It's truly helped."

Sara rubbed his upper arm and smiled. "Sometimes the police have a bad reputation for not listening to people. I pride myself on putting victims' families first, maybe that's because I've been in your position myself."

"I'm grateful that you and your partner are working on my daughter's case."

They followed him back out into the shop. Sara shook his hand. "I hope we don't let you down."

"I have more faith in your abilities than I have in myself overcoming my loss."

"Take care, sir. I'll be in touch very soon."

Sara and Carla left the shop and rounded the corner. Sara paused for a moment, leaned her backside against the wall and put her hands on her knees.

Carla placed a hand on her back. "Oh fuck! Are you all right?"

"I will be. That conversation took a lot out of me. I've pushed down the feelings I once had for Philip, not wanting to hurt Mark, but speaking to Mr Load… all the emotions came flooding back. I feel bloody drained."

"Poor you. Shall we have a drink somewhere to help you recover?"

"Good idea. There's a coffee shop just around the corner that I go to sometimes."

Once Sara was upright again, Carla surprised her by linking arms with her. She smiled at her partner. "You're a good woman, Carla."

"That makes two of us. I'm buying the drinks, it was my suggestion after all. How about a nice sticky cake to go with it?"

Sara laughed. "Now you're spoiling me."

"You're worth spoiling, Sara, you're one in a million."

"Get out of here."

Over coffee, Sara felt a twinge of guilt, knowing what she knew about Carla's ex and not revealing the truth to her after the praise Carla had just bestowed upon her.

"So we have two tough cases on our hands to deal with now. How do you foresee that panning out? Are you going to split the team up?"

"I'd rather not, but it could very well come to that. Enough about work for a moment, how are things with you? Have you been keeping out of trouble lately?" Sara grinned.

"Yeah. What happened a few weeks ago still lingers in my mind. I wish I knew who the fucker was that worked me over. I'd nail the bastard to a post, whip him to within an inch of his life and leave him there for the stray dogs to feast on his flesh and bones."

Sara stared down at the coffee choux bun in her hand and dropped it on the plate. "Thanks for that image and for turning my stomach at the same time."

"Bugger, I thought you had a stronger resolve than that, sorry." Carla continued to eat her pastry without a second thought.

"You carry on, don't let me stop you."

Carla swallowed her mouthful and wiped the excess cream away from her mouth. "I will. Going back to the cases, which one is going to be a priority for us?"

Sara shrugged and took a sip of her coffee before she responded,

"Both have their merits for needing our expertise to be thrown at them. Let me ask you which you think we should prioritise."

Carla dwelled on the question while she finished her mouthful. "Hard to know, I was hoping you'd make the right call and I would follow your lead. That's why you're an inspector and I'm a lowly sergeant."

"Passing the buck, eh? I think we should see how things go for now. I suppose we're going to be more reliant on Lorraine with both cases, maybe what she comes up with will be the incentive we need to put one of the cases before the other one. Damn, even saying that aloud galls me."

"I know how much you like to throw yourself into a case, it's definitely a tough call to make. I don't envy your position one iota."

Sara picked up her cup of coffee and stared at her partner. "That's helpful. Thanks. Let's just go along with the leads we have at present and see where we end up. Have you finished stuffing your face now?"

Carla shoved the final large piece of choux in her mouth and pointed at Sara's half-eaten pastry. "What about you?"

"Say that again, I didn't quite hear you. Wait, no, spare me. Didn't your mother ever tell you how rude it is to speak with your mouth full?"

Carla swallowed what was in her mouth and growled at her, "Uncalled for, you know I have impeccable manners usually."

"Except where luscious cakes are concerned, is that what you're saying?"

Her partner tutted and reached across the table for Sara's plate. "I missed out on breakfast, do you want that or not?"

"By all means, knock yourself out, partner."

Sara watched as Carla demolished what was left of her own pastry that she hadn't had the stomach to eat. "Blimey, not sure where you put it sometimes. The amount you eat and yet you never seem to put on an extra ounce."

"I burn the calories off in other ways."

Sara tilted her head and asked, "Really? Are you telling me you've got another fella on the go and he's a red hot lover between the sheets?"

Carla pulled a face. "No. I've told you, I'm off men for life now after the Gary debacle. What I meant was my adrenaline eats up the calories, well, that and my trips to the gym every other day."

"Wow, get you. It's clearly working if you can shove all that down your neck without gaining any excess weight. Come on, we should be going."

Five minutes later, they left the café and returned to the car. As promised, the girl at the kiosk in Tesco's let them off the parking fee.

Sara drove to the hospital and parked in one of the small roads nearby. They walked through the main entrance and stopped at the reception area. The middle-aged woman with large framed spectacles smiled as they approached.

"Can I help?"

Sara flashed her ID. "We'd like a word with Jack Scott, he's a porter here, if that's possible?"

"I see. I'll have to ring his boss, make sure he's not booked up with any emergency transfers or anything of that nature; our porters are in demand all day long. Why don't you have a seat over there for now? It could take me a little while to track him down."

"Do your best for us, please."

They moved to the waiting area and Sara watched the woman make the call.

"Something doesn't feel right to me," Carla whispered beside her.

"Me neither. Let's give her a few minutes to come up with the goods before we take further action."

"It's your call."

The woman hung up the phone and smiled over at them. "Sorry to keep you waiting, he'll be down shortly. As suspected, he's taking someone from the operating theatre back to the ward."

"Thanks. Roughly, how long?"

"Ten minutes at the most. There's a vending machine in the shop, if you want a drink while you're waiting."

Sara waved her hand in front of her. "We've not long had one."

The receptionist got back to her work.

"I guess our instincts were wrong about her," Sara mumbled.

"Yeah, maybe. Let's not count our chickens too soon. He hasn't appeared yet."

Reaching for one of the magazines on the table, Sara pretended to read while keeping one eye on the receptionist and one eye on the lift.

Carla got out her phone and scrolled through it. "I picked up a new game. Do I have your permission to have a little tinker while we're waiting?"

"Do what you want. What is it?"

"A building block game. You have to build a line and make it disappear."

"Sounds exhilarating! Too much excitement for my blood."

"Cheeky sod. It's relaxing. I either play that or Mahjong for my sins. It really helps me to unwind at the end of the day."

"I'll take your word for that."

"Don't knock something unless you've tried it at least once."

Sara placed a hand on her chest and sighed heavily. "If only I had the time."

"I can sense when someone is mocking me, you know."

A young man in a blue uniform appeared and walked up to the receptionist.

"We're on," Sara said out of the corner of her mouth. She threw the magazine on the table and rose from her seat as the young man turned to face them. Not giving him a chance to bolt, Sara raced forward and smiled at the young man with auburn-coloured, shoulder-length hair. "Jack Scott, I presume?"

"That's right. And you are?"

Sara produced her warrant card and he examined it thoroughly. "DI Sara Ramsey and DS Carla Jameson. We'd like a quick chat with you, if you have the time?"

"The boss has told me to grab a quick break. If you don't mind sitting with me while I have a coffee and a sandwich."

"Suits us."

He pointed at the shop and then at a few tables outside. "Grab a seat, I won't be long. I can't offer to buy you a drink as I'm on a tight budget."

"We're not expecting you to buy us a drink. We'll be waiting for you here." Sara chose the chair facing the shop so she could keep an eye on his progress.

He slipped inside, picked up a sandwich from the fridge and popped a coin into the vending machine. He rejoined them at the table and tore open his sandwich. "What's this about?" He took a bite of his lunch and spilt some lettuce scraps on the table. He gathered them up and shoved them in his mouth.

Sara cringed at the number of germs that were now on their way to mess with his guts. "Your ex-girlfriend."

He grinned and took another bite, and then said, "Which one? I have dozens of them."

Sara raised an eyebrow. "Popular young man then, are you?"

"I have my moments. Most of them pleasurable, if you get my drift."

"I do. There's no need for you to elaborate further. What about Mona, have you seen her recently?"

He paused for a split second and then ploughed on. "Not seen hide nor hair of her, not for a few months."

"Since she dumped you, is that what you're telling us?"

"We parted company. No bitch dumps me." His eyes narrowed as his gaze met Sara's.

"Bitch? Is that how you refer to all your exes?"

He tore another chunk out of his sandwich and chewed for a second or two. "Not really, just the mean ones."

"She was mean to you? How did that manifest itself?"

He stared at his cup of coffee as he answered, "I was down on my luck and she kicked me into touch when I needed her the most."

"That must have made you angry."

"At the time, it did. I was furious. One of my mates stepped in to help me out. If he hadn't, I would have been calling a cardboard box my home by now."

"When was the last time you saw Mona?"

"Not for a while. Look, what's this all about? She's my past, I've moved on. If she's been telling tales on me, then I have a right to know what she's been saying."

"She hasn't." Sara despised his attitude so much that she decided he deserved to be shot down in flames. "We've been told that you found it hard to let her go."

His nose wrinkled and his lip curled up at the side. "Someone's been feeding you a lot of bullshit."

"Really? So you didn't hang around outside her flat, hoping to see her after you'd split up?"

"Didn't you hear me? Someone has been telling lies about me. Why would I hang around that bitch's place when she refused to even speak to me?"

"You tried to call her?"

"Only a few times after she tricked me and locked me out of the house. How callous can someone you thought you knew be? I was in a desperate situation and she threw the towel in instead of helping me out. I could never do that to another person."

"Sorry to hear that. You've moved on now, you're settled again somewhere else? With another woman perhaps?"

"No. I'm still sleeping in my friend's spare room. He's been good to me. We get on great, he's told me to stay as long as I need to and I'm going to take him up on that."

"You still sound bitter from the whole experience."

"Wouldn't you be? I thought I had something with Mona, we'd been seeing each other for around five months, then one day she bloody locked me out of her flat and refused to speak to me."

"No reasons given?"

He sighed and his expression darkened. "No. I wish I knew why, maybe we would've been able to overcome what had gone wrong between us."

"And you would have been willing to have done that?"

"Yes, I loved her. Wait, I think I was in love with her."

Sara frowned. "You're not sure?"

"It felt like love. Hard to tell when you've never had those types of feelings for someone before. I'm not likely to in the future either, after the way it was shoved back in my face by Mona."

"Relationships can be complicated and need to be handled carefully at times."

"You're not kidding. Which is why I've decided to steer clear of women for a while. I'm so much better now, you know, more settled. I'm having a blast being single again, why would I want to change things? Anyway, you've asked enough questions about me and yet, you still haven't told me why you're here."

"The thing is… Mona was found dead today." She came right out and said it, eager to see what his reaction would be to the devastating news.

He slumped back in his chair and stared at Sara. His sandwich flopped out of his hand onto the paper bag it came in. Stunned, he shook his head, and his mouth opened and closed a few times as he grappled for the right words to say.

"Are you all right?" Sara asked after a few telling moments.

"I'm in shock. Are you sure it was her? She was so young. How did it happen? Was she involved in an accident?"

"I'm sorry, no, she was killed."

"Wh… what? I can't believe I'm hearing this. Who would want to kill…? Wait, I get it now! Jesus, you're here questioning me because you believe I did this. I swear I didn't. I don't have it in me to kill another person. You've got this all wrong."

His voice escalated, drawing attention from the other customers sitting at the nearby tables around them. "Try to remain calm. After speaking with you, no, I don't believe you're guilty of the crime. Although we're going to need to seek an alibi for you, just to keep the paperwork tidy."

"Thank fuck for that. I've heard so many horror stories where the police tried to pin a murder on an innocent person, usually a husband or boyfriend, or ex-boyfriend should I say. Bloody hell, I'm sorry for calling her a bitch, I never would have done that had I known that she was dead."

"I believe you. Try to keep calm. I need you to think back, during your time with her, did Mona ever have any problems with other men? Someone stalking her, perhaps?"

"No, not that she told me about. God, is that what happened to her? Someone followed her and killed her? Why, why would someone do that to such a bright and bubbly person?"

"That's what we're trying to find out."

"Do you know it was a man who killed her?"

Sara glanced around her and then leaned forward and whispered, "She was also raped. But that part isn't likely to come out in the news."

His hands slapped against his cheeks, and he appeared dumbfounded by the information. "Oh, God, that's just awful. So she really suffered before her death." He closed his eyes. "I don't want to imagine her going through that."

"It is appalling. If you can think of anything that you believe might help us, will you get in touch?" Sara slid a card across the table, bypassing his discarded sandwich.

"I promise I will. Bloody hell, I want this person caught as much as you do." He shook his head a few times. "Why?" He repeated the word over and over.

"We've yet to establish the whys and wherefores. We're going to head off now. I'm sorry to have dropped this bombshell on you like this, during your shift."

"It's fine. I'd rather know from you than hear about this through the media. Please, please get this bastard and punish him for robbing us of this beautiful girl. Yes, she had her faults, but don't we all?"

"We do indeed. Take care."

Jack nodded. "I will."

Sara and Carla left the hospital and made their way back to the car. "You believed him then?" Carla asked.

Sara shot her a glance. "Didn't you?"

Carla chewed her lip before answering, "I'm not so sure. I'm willing to go along with your perception of the guy on this one because, in truth, I just couldn't work him out."

"Fair enough. I get occasions like that with some people I question as well. He seemed to be too cut up to me."

"Cut up? He came across as angry to me."

"That as well. I'll tell you what, just in case my gut feeling is way off the mark with him, we'll keep him on the suspect list for now."

They reached the car. Carla looked over the roof at her. "I'd feel happier if we did that. Thanks, Sara."

"For what? Listening to my astute partner? Get in the car, and I repeat, don't ever feel bad about speaking out if something doesn't gel with you."

They slipped into the vehicle. "That's a deal. What now?"

"Back to the station and start the investigation now we've contacted the next of kin and who we should logically note as the main suspect."

"What if this was a one-off, an attack by a stranger? How the hell are we going to track down the culprit?"

Sara pulled out of the road and joined the traffic which had ground to a halt at the lights. "That's the sixty-four-thousand-dollar question right there. I sense solving this case is going to be tougher than most we've had to deal with lately."

5

"What's going on, guys?" Sara demanded, hearing the commotion that awaited their arrival in the incident room.

"Sorry about the noise, boss. I was thrilled to find something on CCTV and needed to share it with the others," Craig replied, looking sheepish.

After nodding her understanding, Sara pointed at the screen on his desk. "Well, you'd better show me then."

He settled back into his seat and hit a few keys while Sara pulled up a chair and sat alongside him, her gaze drawn to his monitor.

"Here. This black Peugeot was parked close to the entrance of the alley just before Mona's body was discovered."

"How long was it there?" Sara asked, her interest skyrocketing.

"I've gone back and forth several times, it was positioned there around thirty minutes in total."

"Enough time to wait for Mona to arrive and then kill her. I don't suppose you got a close-up on the driver either in the vehicle or when he left it?"

"No close up, but this is him exiting the car and heading towards the alley. As you can see, he's doing his best to disguise himself, wearing a cap and pulling up the collar on his coat."

"Okay, it's quite a distinctive coat nevertheless. Once we pick him up for questioning, if we ever get that far, we can search his property for the coat and cap and match them to the CCTV. Teaching you how to suck eggs, I know, it's just me thinking out loud."

Craig grinned. "I thought the same, boss."

"Right, keep up the good work, Craig. Let me know if you stumble across the reg number."

"I'll do that, nothing so far, but I'll keep digging. If this proves pointless, I'll try and source footage from elsewhere and then try to track the car through the ANPRs."

She stood and squeezed his shoulder. "Good man."

Sara then brought the whiteboard up to date. Carla handed her a coffee. She'd almost finished her task when DCI Carol Price entered the room. The euphoria from moments earlier died down, and a hush descended.

"As you were, team, don't let my presence prevent you from working. DI Ramsey, can I see you in your office?" She marched into the office ahead of Sara.

Sara cast a glance in Carla's direction and shrugged. She entered the room a few seconds later to find DCI Price already seated. Sara closed the door and sat in her chair. "Something wrong, ma'am?"

"I don't know, is there? Am I not allowed to do the rounds now and again?"

"Of course you are. I always get nervous when you make a special trip to see me and don't summon me to your office."

"That'll be your guilty conscience prodding you then, right?"

"I wouldn't put it quite like that. My conscience is perfectly clear, this week at least."

"I'm glad to hear it. I wondered if you'd made your decision yet."

Sara was aware of what the chief was referring to, but decided to play innocent. "Sorry?"

"Don't bullshit a bullshitter, Sara Ramsey. You were given a very important task to do within a certain deadline. Have you made your decision, yes or no?"

"Sorry, but no. At present, we're working two murders. Yes, you heard me right, *two* murders. If I let one of my team go now, can you imagine the pressure that's going to put the rest of them under?"

"While I appreciate your side of the argument, I have Head Office jumping up and down on my neck, so to speak. Needs must, Sara, we *need* to get this actioned immediately. I've allowed you to stall long enough and now is the time to give me a name."

Sara shook her head adamantly. "Why don't we throw my name into the hat, how's that?"

Carol's eyes widened. "Don't be so ridiculous, woman."

"Am I? You're sitting here, asking me to throw a bloody member of my team under the bus, how the hell do you expect me to react?"

"With professionalism. As I said before, this is part and parcel of your role as an Inspector. You need to take your duties seriously."

"Really? You think I play at this role every day of my life? I'm surrounded by excellent people who give me their bloody all while they're here. I can't, no, I won't do it. If by going against your orders, I get the boot, then so be it. I'd rather get the sack myself than see an excellent member of my team shafted when they've done nothing wrong."

"While I admire your loyalty, your pride, or obstinacy should I say, is pissing me off, Sara."

"I have no regrets in that matter, ma'am. I'm not prepared to cut the staff, not now and not in the future. When I look around this station, it's clear to me where staff can be cut—the number of times I see certain officers outside having a sneaky fag."

"They're entitled to their break, just like anyone else."

"I'm not saying I begrudge that, I'm merely pointing out that it seems to be the same people swinging the lead all the time."

"I'll look into it. The trouble is, it's your department or team that has been targeted by Head Office."

"Fine. Then it's up to you to make them see sense. Did you miss the part where *my team* are working two separate murder cases at the moment? Look around you, name me another team worthy of doing that in this station. In the bloody county!" She bit back, her voice rising to a squeak.

"Will you calm down? Stop talking to me as if I'm one of your team and start treating me like your superior officer."

Sara slumped back in her chair. "They're the facts, ma'am. I'm sick to death of laying the facts on the table for you, especially when you choose to ignore what I tell you."

"For your information, I have *never* ignored you when you've spoken. I know you're passionate about this, Sara, but give me a break, please."

She bounced forward again. "Me, give you a break? It should be the other way around, ma'am. You've had my final word on the matter, when do you want my resignation on your desk?"

DCI Price flew out of her chair and marched out of the room without bothering to answer.

Sara made an imaginary strike in the air with her finger. "One to me."

Carla appeared in the doorway, looking miffed. "Everything all right?"

"Come in. I wasn't going to tell you, but I think the time has come to share the news."

"Crap! Sounds ominous. Are you in trouble?"

"I could well be if my ploy doesn't work out."

Her partner frowned. "Ploy?"

"Yes. Last month, the DCI came to me with orders from above to cut staff."

"Isn't that the norm in the force? They're always trying to police with the bare minimum, aren't they?"

"You're missing the point here, Carla. Our team has been specifically targeted, not the station in general. Us!"

Carla winced. "Ouch, sorry, I'm a bit slow on the uptake." Her voice lowered. "What are you going to do?"

"I can't possibly put anyone's name in the hat, you know how well everyone works around here, we all play a valuable part in a well-oiled machine. I inherited a fabulous team who have accepted me with open arms, how can I sack one of them for fuck's sake? I just can't."

"You're going to have to. What's the alternative?"

"The chief reminded me in no uncertain terms that it's my responsibility to manage the team on all levels."

"Meaning you get to pick someone to fire. Shit! That sucks."

"You're telling me."

"Is that why she stormed out?"

"That and the fact that I asked her when she wanted my resignation letter."

"You *didn't*? You called her bluff?"

Sara picked up a pen and tapped it against her cheek. "I did. I can't be dealing with shit like this. Look at today for instance, my mind should be on the *two* murder investigations we're running. I reminded her that we're the only team dealing with two such cases, but it didn't make the slightest difference. So, I let her have it."

"Sara, Sara, Sara, what have you done?"

She paused the pen and stared at Carla. "What any self-respecting inspector would do in my situation, I'm presuming."

Carla groaned. "You think? I doubt if anyone would be as crazy as you."

"Crazy, is that what you really think of me?"

"And some. You're a loveable lunatic though, if that helps."

They both laughed, cutting through the tension.

"Anyway, let's not dwell on the issue, and I'm relying on you to keep this close to your chest. I'll tell the team, if and when, the time is right."

"You have my word. These things are sent to try us, as they say."

"Don't they just? Back to the investigation. How is Craig getting on?"

"You'll have to ask him. He keeps whooping now and again, but isn't willing to share what he's found so far. I think he's waiting for you to get back to him. I think he has a soft spot for you."

"No, don't be daft." Sara felt her cheeks warm.

"I've seen the way he looks at you. He hangs on your every word whenever you engage him in conversation."

Sara snorted and chuckled for a few seconds until tears formed. "You're a scream. I think you're winding me up."

Carla laughed. "Maybe I am. Made you laugh though."

"You did that. Come on, I've had enough of sitting in this office, let's see what the team have managed to find out in my absence."

They went back into the incident room and Sara did the rounds, leaving Craig until the end of her journey. "Hi, Craig, do you have an update for me?"

"Yes, boss. I've got several clips lined up for you. One that is going to blow your mind."

Sara suppressed a giggle trying to emerge as she noted the excitement in his voice. "Let me see."

He replayed several clips of the man leaving his vehicle and returning to it in a hurry. The car drove off and that's when it was plain to see the reg number of the vehicle. "Shit. We've got him. Do a search on that number, Craig."

"Already done it, boss. The car belongs to a Jo Zappel of Windsor Road."

"Boss, I have something of interest that has just been highlighted on my screen," Christine shouted.

"I'll be back," she told Craig and darted across the other side of the room. "Tell me more, Christine."

"It's regarding Val Purcell's account. The bank has been in touch to tell me that someone withdrew three hundred pounds from the woman's account."

"Wow, okay. So the trap worked, or has it? What have they done about it?"

"They let the payment go through as instructed, they also sent me this footage from the ATM." She tapped Enter on her keyboard and up popped an image that blew Sara's mind.

"What the…? Craig, get over here, now!"

He came to a sliding stop beside her and let out a long, low whistle that affected her hearing. "Jesus, it's him. The same bloke."

"As I suspected. You know what that means, don't you?"

Craig frowned and shook his head. "No, what am I missing?"

Sara groaned. "Both cases are connected. We're looking for the same perp for both murders." She fist-pumped the air. "Now, all we need to do is find the bastard and bring him in."

"Well, we've got his address. Want me to send a patrol car to see if his vehicle is there?" Craig suggested.

"No, Carla and I will go. We'll take backup with us, any volunteers?"

Craig grinned broadly and raised his hand. "I'm up for it, boss."

Sara shot Carla a glance, and her partner stifled a grin and looked away.

"Anyone else? Preferably male, as we might need to use force to bring him in. What about you, Will?"

"Why not?" he shrugged.

"Right, let's go then. Craig, give Carla the address. I'll nip and get my coat."

The four of them left the office and bolted down the stairs. DCI Price was coming up at the same time.

"Hey, what's the rush? You're acting like a gang of children running through the school corridors," the chief called after them.

Without stopping or looking back, Sara shouted, "Have to fly. I'll fill you in when we get back."

"Make sure you do," the chief replied.

Once they were in the car, Carla snapped on her seatbelt and stated, "You could have stopped to fill her in. Whizzing past her like that isn't going to make the situation any better... just saying."

"I know." Sara laughed and revved the car. "But it felt bloody good doing it."

"You're nuts."

"What can I say? I love living on the edge when it suits, and boy, does it suit right now? There's a reason I chose not to stop and fill her in."

"Which is?"

Sara eased out of the car park once Carla had set the satnav route.

"Because as far as she knows, we're dealing with two cases. If I tell her we suspect the cases are linked, then she could turn up the pressure on me again. This way, it gives me breathing space and I can concentrate on the investigation instead of sitting at my desk weighing up the rights and wrongs about why I need to sack someone. Anyway, I've lobbed the ball back in her direction, so it's up to her to sort something out for the good of the team. If she chooses to accept my resignation, then so be it. There's very little I can do to alter her mind."

"Don't say that. I couldn't work with anyone else. Not as well as I work with you, Sara."

"As much as I love hearing you say that, if it comes to the crunch, then I will go through with my threat. I'm a woman of my word, I rarely go back on it, hon. You should know that by now."

"What you're really saying there is that you're stubborn with a capital S."

"That as well. Less chat about what might be in our near future, we have a suspect to apprehend, a dangerous killer in fact."

*S*ara pulled up outside the house they were after and motioned for Craig and Will to remain in the vehicle. Her mobile rang, it was Craig. "You want us to stay put, boss?"

"Yes, Craig, for now. Let me and Carla do the talking. Keep vigilant; any sign of trouble, you can come to our rescue, not before that, you hear me?"

"That's a roger, boss."

Sara ended the call and shook her head when she caught Carla smirking. "Am I going to have to contend with this from now on?"

"Soft spot, that's all I'm saying."

"He also has a girlfriend he's about to pop the question to, if I recall rightly... just saying."

"That doesn't mean he doesn't fancy you as well."

"Get a life, Carla. Come on, let's start taking things seriously. Pepper spray in hand on this one, shove it up your sleeve if necessary."

"I know the drill."

"*On y va*, as the French would say."

Carla yanked her back, preventing her from getting out of the vehicle. "Did you just swear at me in a foreign language?"

"Not at all. On we go, it means. You need to broaden your horizons in life, love."

"Whatever."

They approached the front door of the shabby-looking terraced property, watching their step en route up the craggy concrete path. Sara prepared herself by sucking in a few calming breaths. She rang the doorbell and withdrew her ID from her coat pocket.

The door opened. A man in his fifties, with greying hair and the start of a beard darkening on his chin, stood on the threshold. "Yeah, what do you want?"

"Jo Zappel?"

He seemed perplexed. "Has the landlord sent you? I know I'm behind on the rent, but things have been a little tough lately. I'm doing my best to find funds, but it's proving difficult."

"Ah, no. We're not from the landlord." Sara placed her warrant card in front of his face and heard him gulp. "DI Sara Ramsey and DS Carla Jameson. We'd like you to accompany us to the station, sir."

"For what? Er… you can't come to my house demanding this, that and the other, you just can't."

"I'm afraid we can if we have reason to believe you're guilty of a serious crime or two, or three… who knows at this stage?"

He frowned, quickly stepped back and tried to slam the door in their faces. Carla was the first to react. She slammed both her hands into the door, it shot back and sent the man off balance. Carla followed the movement up by pouncing on him and placing cuffs on his wrists before he could say or do anything else. She yanked him to his feet. His head swivelled between Sara and Carla.

"I'm telling you, I ain't done nothing wrong," Zappel protested.

Craig and Will got out of their car and headed towards them.

"Hand him over, Carla. They can take him back to base."

"Oi, what about my cat? She's in the house, who's going to feed her?"

"I'll pop in there and fill her bowl for a few days," Sara suggested.

"Yeah, I know the drill. Think you're doing me a favour when all the time you've just gained free access to my house. Nope, she can starve for all I care."

"Your choice, Zappel. We'll have a search warrant within a few hours, anyway. You really want your precious cat to starve?"

"No. Feed her then. I'll be back before I know it, because I won't be able to tell you nothin'."

"We'll see about that. Do you need anything else from the house?"

"My hat and coat, they're on the hook behind the door in the hallway."

Sara marched into the house and unhooked the black coat and cap which he'd been wearing in the CCTV footage and went back outside. "Are these yours?"

"Yes, they're mine."

Sara exchanged a triumphant glance with the other three officers. "Good."

Craig slung the coat and cap in an evidence bag. Sara went back inside to fetch another jacket for the suspect.

"Ere, you can't do that," Zappel shouted, frowning. Craig and Will ignored the suspect and put him in the back of their vehicle.

Sara and Carla waited for the car to set off and then went into the house. "You do realise we could be in the wrong here, don't you?" Carla asked.

"No, not when he gave us permission to enter the house to feed the cat. We'll do that, have a quick snoop around and be out of here before you can say 'the cat ate the goldfish when I wasn't looking'."

"Funny ha ha! What if he doesn't have a goldfish?" Carla chuckled.

Sara smirked and they entered the front room. Sara's nose wrinkled. "Anyway, we have the hat and coat as pretty rigid evidence. Not the most pleasant smell I've ever bloody encountered. Sweaty socks and takeaways, what a vile combination." She pointed at the corner of the room where a mound of different food cartons filled the space.

"Jesus, what a fucking pig," Carla uttered.

"Nope, pigs are supposed to be clean animals, unlike this cretin. There's no sign of a cat in here, I'll go through to the kitchen." Sara went past a tired old sleeping bag on the couch, not bearing to look too closely at the stains on the dark blue cover in case it finished her stomach off.

A friendly black and white pussy came to greet her, and it weaved in and out of her legs as she crossed the room to look under the sink for its food. That's where she kept Misty's meals at home. "Hello, sweetie. Are you hungry?" Sara peered in the cat's bowl on the kitchen windowsill and retched. The thing hadn't been washed out in decades by the look of it. She opened a few of the cupboards on the wall and removed a side plate that had a huge crack in it. Next, she hunted through the cutlery drawer to find a can opener. It was rusty as hell, but eventually, with a vast amount of patience, she opened enough of the can to remove half the food. She mashed it with a spoon and offered it to the starving cat. "He clearly doesn't tend to your every need, does he, sweetheart?"

"Not your problem before you go getting any ideas," Carla said from the doorway.

"I know. I'll place a call to the RSPCA, see if they'll come and pick it up."

"Want me to go take a sneaky peek upstairs?"

"We'll both go. Let's leave this one to enjoy her meal in peace."

Upstairs, there were two doors. One led into the bathroom and the other into the main bedroom. If they thought the lounge was a mess, it was nothing compared to the bedroom. "Christ, what is wrong with people? This place is disgusting and no, I have no intention of venturing into the bathroom to bloody see what's in there. The smell is even worse up here. I'm getting a headache from an odour and I can't even begin to guess where the damn smell is coming from." She pointed at the unmade bed with the filthy sheet spread across the mattress. "I suspect that's the culprit, but I have no intention of getting up close and personal with it to give it the once over."

Carla nodded and gagged. She cupped her hand over her nose and mouth and murmured, "I never thought I hear myself say this, but I wish I had one of those damn masks handy. The pandemic has nothing on this shithole."

"I agree. Let's get out of here. Leave SOCO to it once we get the warrant sorted."

They rushed down the stairs and closed the front door behind them. Both of them inhaled lungfuls of fresh air while they made their way back to the car. Sara threw Carla the keys to her car. "Here, you drive, I want to make a few calls on the way."

"Wow, that's a first. You, trusting me with your baby."

"It's actually the second time I've allowed you behind the wheel, but who's counting?"

Carla adjusted her seat and then revved the engine.

"Umm... less of that, if you don't mind. I've always driven her carefully and with respect, I'm trusting you to do the same."

"All right, I was only teasing. It's fifty around here, right?"

"No, it bloody well isn't, this is a thirty zone." Sara groaned when Carla grinned. "Get us back to the station safely."

"I will boss, trust me."

Sara removed her mobile from her pocket and looked up the number for the local RSPCA. She gave them Zappel's address and explained the situation. The woman at the other end asked if Zappel had any relatives. "I don't think so. We haven't had a chance to do any digging into his background, as such. Can you deal with the cat for us or not?"

"I'll send an officer out to take a look."

"Thanks. I'll leave it in your capable hands then." Sara ended the call. "Jesus, you'd think they'd be grateful I was looking out for the cat instead of grilling me like that."

"I've heard some bad reports about them lately."

"I'm not going to go there, so have I, but I thought I'd give them the benefit of the doubt. I hope I don't live to regret that decision. Maybe I'll drop round there in a couple of days, to check on the cat. It's such a sweet thing, despite having a murderer for its owner. It's hardly the cat's fault, is it?"

"Don't get involved, Sara."

"Too late. I will never knowingly stand back and watch an animal in need suffer. If I have to take it home with me, I will."

"I knew those words would tumble out of your mouth, eventually. How would Misty feel about the intrusion?"

"She's a gem. I'm sure she'd be fine about it."

"Are you willing to take the risk? Aren't cats supposed to be territorial animals?"

Sara scratched her head. "Are they? Anyway, that's pie in the sky at the moment. I need to make another call. She dialled a number she had stored in her phone and arranged for a warrant to be actioned for Zappel's address. The woman she spoke to said they had a slew of applications to go through and it could be at least forty-eight hours before one was actioned. Sara sighed and ended the call. "It's not just us who are overwhelmed by the sounds of it. Two bloody days we're going to have to wait."

"We're going to be busy interviewing the suspect so it shouldn't make a difference, not really."

Carla indicated and pulled into the main car park at the station. Sara got out and inspected her parking. "Something wrong?"

Sara grinned. "You're a little too close to the line on this side for my liking."

Carla flung the keys across the roof of the car. "You could always park it yourself."

Sara pulled a face and refrained from poking her tongue out. "You can buy the coffees for your insubordination."

"Get you spouting a big word in the middle of the day."

They laughed and walked into the station.

Jeff glanced up from behind his reception desk. "Nice to see someone smiling."

"We have every reason to smile, Jeff. We've caught a suspect without breaking out in a sweat, within days of him committing the first crime."

Jeff clapped his hands. "So I hear. Another notch on your belt, Inspector Ramsey."

"Is he ready to interview?"

"He should be soon. He's still being processed by the custody sergeant."

"We'll be upstairs, having a caffeine fix, ring me when he's been cleared and the duty solicitor gets here."

"I'll do that."

DCI Price was standing at the top of the stairs, waiting for Sara. "Do you have time for that chat now?"

"I was hoping to grab a coffee before I start interviewing a suspect, boss."

Carol turned and walked into the incident room, which fell silent upon her arrival. Sara and Carla followed. Carla veered off to the vending machine. Sara motioned for the DCI to join her in her office. Before either of them had sat down, Carla appeared with two cups of coffee.

"Drink that at your own risk," Sara chuckled. "It's nothing compared to what you're used to drinking."

"If it's wet and strong, then it'll do the trick. Thanks, Carla," the chief said with a taut smile.

Sara winked at her partner. "Can you close the door on the way out?"

Carla did as instructed. Sara stared at the chief, expecting her to state why she was there. When she didn't, Sara asked, "Everything all right, boss?"

"I hear you have a suspect in custody. I take it you were going to let me know at some stage, Inspector."

"Umm... am I supposed to? In time, yes, but the second I step back into the station and before I've had the chance to fire a single question at the man?"

"All right, point taken. I presume you would have got around to it, eventually."

"Too right, I would have. I wasn't aware that I had to inform you of my every move. I must have missed that directive when it came down from Head Office."

"Don't you dare use that sarcastic tone with me, Inspector."

Sara was confused by the chief's overzealous reaction. "What's going on, boss? You sound peeved with me. May I ask why?"

"Not really. Oh, I don't know. Maybe I'm guilty of taking my bad mood out on you. I'm sorry."

"Bad mood?"

"I tried to fight your corner for you, I swear I did, but I failed. No one at Head Office is prepared to listen to what I have to say on the cuts. In fact, I stirred up a hornet's nest and now they're insisting we give them a name by the end of the week."

"That's utter bollocks. Do they realise the intense pressure I'm going to be under in the next few days with a suspect sitting in the holding cells?"

"I think they're perfectly aware of what goes on in our everyday lives."

"Seriously? I doubt that much is true. They haven't got a damn clue what stress we're under from one day to the next. It pisses me off, a lot. To think we're busting a gut, putting our lives on the line every single day, only to have this type of shit flung at us. I've had it."

"Don't overreact, Sara. You're going to need to calm down. I've got your back and I promise, I'm still doing all I can to reverse the decision."

"In the meantime, I'm expected to carry out my serious job while having someone's future on my conscience. How do you expect me to deal with that type of stress, boss?"

"I appreciate how difficult all of this is for you, Sara, but it comes with the territory."

Sara fell silent and sipped at her drink without uttering another word in case the wrong thing slipped out.

"Say something," Carol demanded.

Sara hitched up a weary shoulder. "I'm done. I have nothing left to say on the subject because, to be honest, what's the point? All we're doing is going round and round in circles. It's wearing me out. I can't be arsed with all this bullshit bureaucracy any more. I told you this morning, the decision has to be yours, I refuse to throw one of my *excellent* detectives under the guillotine. Now, if you'll excuse me, I have a very dangerous suspect to interview." She downed her drink and pushed back her chair. The chief stared at her open-mouthed. Sara walked past her and cringed as she reached for the door handle.

"Stop right there. You leave this office and you might as well pack up your stuff and say goodbye to your career and the pension you've paid into."

Sara closed her eyes. Realising, for the first time, she had overstepped the mark with her relatively new boss.

"Sit down. I'll tell you when you can leave this office."

Sara dragged her feet like a four-year-old child and plonked down in her chair once more. She opened her mouth to apologise, but the chief raised her hand to silence her.

"I think you've said enough, don't you? I'm sick to death of you venting your bloody anger on me. Don't shoot the ruddy messenger, lady. How many more times do I have to tell you I'm on your side? I've done all I can without putting my own job on the line to save someone else's role on this team. These are tough times, surely you realise that?"

"I…" Sara began, but the chief glared at her, silencing her tongue.

"I don't want to hear it. I'm fed up with you fighting me on this one, Sara. I've always considered you a pleasure to work with, until this particular conundrum started prodding us with a stick. I'm not the enemy, kindly remember that. I'm here to speak to you as a team member. To try and find a suitable solution that we can take back to Head Office."

Sara raised her hand. "Permission to speak?"

"Don't be childish!"

"I'm not."

"Speak, make it worth listening to."

"What are you suggesting by that, some sort of job share?"

The chief nodded. "If it comes down to it, yes. I believe Head Office would compromise if that option was put forward."

Sara contemplated the development that had surfaced. "It might work. It's difficult to say how it's going to go down when I have to keep schtum about it."

"I'm betting you've run this past Carla, don't deny it if it's true."

"Only this morning, I'd kept it quiet until then. She's as shocked as I am."

"Maybe she knows something that you don't."

"Excuse me? I'm not sure what you're getting at."

"Carla knows the other team members better than you, perhaps she's aware of their personal circumstances. What if a couple of the ladies on the team are thinking of having a child? It might be the solution to the problem."

"Couldn't that be classed as a sexist statement to make? What if some of the men were thinking of going down that route?"

The chief tipped her head back and sighed. "You're missing the point."

"Am I? I don't think I am."

"Maybe that was the wrong choice of scenario on my part. Help me out here, Sara. You know your staff better than I do."

"That's the trouble, I don't. I turn up here to do my shift and work my butt off. I haven't got a clue how many kids some members of the team have, even if half of them are married or not. Carla's a different story, I'm with her most of the day, but as for the others, I never get the chance to sit down and have a heart to heart with them."

"That's sad, but understandable at the same time. Get Carla in here, let's see what she has to say about the subject."

Sara shook her head. "I think it's grossly unfair to put this on her."

"Do it!"

Sara left her seat and reluctantly shouted for Carla to join them from the doorway. Carla glanced around the incident room at her colleagues, some of whom gave her the thumbs-up. "Have I done something wrong?" Carla mouthed, on her walk towards Sara.

"No. We just want your opinion on something."

She swiped her brow in relief and entered the office. Sara let her pass and then pulled an extra chair into the room.

Carla sat down and asked, "What can I do for you?"

Sara went to the other side of the desk and settled into her chair, then recapped what she and the chief had been discussing.

Carla placed a hand across her chest. "And you're expecting me to break a confidence, is that it?"

"No, that's not how I see it," the chief replied defensively.

Sara suppressed the chuckle bubbling beneath. *You go, girl. Give her hell.*

"Okay, I give up," the chief finally said after ten minutes of getting nowhere, even after Carla entered the room. "Let me mull it over. I need you two to keep the lid on this until I can come up with a viable solution."

"Don't worry, our lips are sealed, aren't they, Carla?"

"Guaranteed." Carla smiled at the chief and jumped out of her seat to let her pass. Once the door was shut, Sara let out the large breath she'd been holding in. "That's twenty minutes I don't plan on revisiting anytime soon."

"I feel for you. What a terrible dilemma to find yourself in, Sara."

"You're not wrong. Save your sympathy for the person who is eventually going to lose their job once this godawful decision has been made."

"Ugh… this is all so unfair."

"Tell me about it. Come on, we've got better things to occupy our time rather than dwell on making a colleague's life a misery. We have a suspect to question."

6

_____

*A*s soon as Sara and Carla joined Zappel and the duty solicitor in the interview room, Sara picked up on the suspect's mood. He appeared to be a broken man—defeated, some might even say.

Carla ran through the verbiage to get the proceedings underway for the recording.

"I'll be calling you Jo, if that's okay?" was the first thing Sara said.

He shrugged. "Whatever suits you." He stared at the table, his head low, avoiding all eye contact.

"Why did you do it, Jo? Why kill that innocent old lady? You got what you wanted, why then take her damn life?"

His watery gaze met hers. "I didn't."

Is that remorse I'm hearing in his tone? His demeanour is remorseful too! What's going on? We've captured him, maybe that was enough to do the trick. Perhaps he's going to admit his guilt, and this is all going to be a doddle.

"Come now." Sara took a crime scene photo from the folder she'd brought with her and slid it across to lay in front of him. "You're expecting me to believe you didn't end this woman's life?"

"I didn't," he said quietly. His gaze averting the photo.

Sara pushed the image to a different part of the table, forcing him to lay his eyes on it. "Go on, look at it. You did this, at least have the courage to see the consequences of your actions. You took this woman's life, leaving me to share the news with her grieving family, and you're sitting there denying it. What kind of fool do you take me for?"

"I'm telling you I didn't do it."

Sara produced another image. This time, it was the CCTV footage from the ATM. Zappel groaned. "Next, you'll be telling me this isn't you."

"It's not."

"I beg to differ. When we removed the same coat and hat from your house earlier, you admitted they belonged to you. Now you're sitting there and denying it?"

"I'm not denying they're mine, I'm denying that's me in the photo." He sat back and folded his arms.

Sara stared, trying to unnerve him. He was a strange subject to work out. "Why? Why are you denying you committed the murder when we have you bang to rights? It's only a matter of time before we hear back from Forensics with any DNA found at the scene. But even when that comes through, the fact that you were seen extracting money from the dead woman's account, as in this picture here, has put the ultimate nail in your coffin. And yes, pun intended. We've got all the proof we need to put you behind bars for a very long time."

"Except, I didn't do it."

Sara mimicked him and folded her arms. "All right, let's play things your way for a while, see where that gets us, shall we? If you didn't do it, then who did?"

"No comment."

Shit! Not what I was expecting at all.

"People usually tend to go down the 'no comment' route when an officer gets close to the truth, is that it, Jo? Am I close to the truth?"

He glanced up, bared his yellow teeth and said, "No comment."

"Okay, we'll move on in that case." She removed another crime scene photo from the file and placed it in front of him.

He stared at the photo for several moments, appearing to be mesmerised by the image. "What can you tell me about the victim?"

His head tilted up and his gaze met hers. There was a look of confusion on his face. "What? Who is this?"

"This, as if you didn't know, is your second victim within the past twenty-four hours."

He shoved the photo away and turned to his solicitor. "No frigging way! I didn't do it. They're not pinning that fucking one on me. Nor the bloody first one, either. I didn't do this, I swear."

"What proof do you have that my client murdered this young woman, Inspector?" Mr Jordan demanded.

"Hmm... let's see. Oh yes, here we have your client's car leaving the murder scene. Next you'll be denying this is your car I take it, Jo."

His head protruded and he stared at the final photo Sara had placed on the table. "What the...? Yes, I'm denying it. Someone must have cloned my car. That's not mine."

"Cloned it?" Sara laughed. "That's funny, I've never heard that one before during an interview. Why on earth would someone do that?"

He folded his arms tighter. "How the fuck should I know? That's *not* my car."

"We'll let the courts decide, shall we? We've impounded your car and ordered a search warrant for your home. You'll be spending time in the cells until you admit to us why you committed these two murders."

"I haven't done anything wrong. You've made a bloody mistake, I'm telling you. Why won't you believe me?"

"The evidence is clear for us all to see."

The solicitor leaned over and whispered something in his ear. Jo sat back and stared at him. "I ain't admitting nothing. This is all bullshit. I'm not admitting to someone else's sins. What do you frigging take me for?"

"If you insist on pleading your innocence, you're only going to make matters worse for yourself once you go before a jury."

He wrung his hands nervously. "That's bollocks, all this is shite I'm telling you."

"Give it up, Jo. We've got all we need to convict you. Why don't you save us all time by admitting you killed these two women and be done with it?"

He leaned forward and shouted, "Because I didn't do this, *any* of it. You've got the wrong person."

"Why tell us we've made a mistake when the evidence is right there, for all to see? This is you withdrawing money from an ATM. We traced the transaction, it led back to Val Purcell's account." Sara tapped the woman's photo. "You'll be telling us next that you're not in possession of her bank card. I'm warning you, don't waste your breath."

"I'm not, and I don't have a clue where the old woman's card is." He growled.

"Why change your MO? Why go from knocking on the old lady's door and killing her in her own home to attacking this young woman down an alley, raping and then murdering her at the scene?"

"What? I fucking did no such thing. I've never raped no one. You cannot pin this one on me. No way!"

Sara watched his body language throughout for any sign she was getting close to the truth. "We'll see what Forensics have to say to prove you wrong. You're here, why not admit your guilt and we can move on? Get you processed and on your way to a comfy prison cell."

"Fuck off. Is this how it works these days? Cops fucking falsifying evidence? Is that how you meet your damn targets?"

"No, and we're not falsifying any evidence. Why won't you admit it? What's to gain from putting up the barriers and denying this is you in this photo?"

"Doh! Let's see... because it's the fucking truth, but you're refusing to accept what I'm telling you."

"All right, let's approach things from a different angle, shall we?"

"Go for it. Because you're not getting very far with the route you've chosen so far, are you?"

Sara narrowed her eyes and stared at him. He was starting to try her patience. She inhaled a deep breath to keep her anger under control and pinned a false smile in place. "Okay, perhaps you can tell me if anyone has access to your car?"

Zappel hesitated before he answered. Then he vehemently shook his head. "Nope. Next?"

"Right, that didn't work. So we're back to square one. We have enough proof to place you at the scene of both c rimes."

"Like fuck you do. Don't give me that bullshit."

"Val Purcell died after an intruder got into her house and robbed her of a stash of cash and apparently her bank card." Sara poked at the ATM photo. "And here, we have you withdrawing extra funds from her account. How did you get hold of her card within a few hours of her death?"

"I didn't. That's not me. It's someone who looks like me."

"Really? Next you'll be telling me that someone is doing their best to fit you up for the crimes." Sara laughed.

"Yep, you've hit the bullseye with that one, babe."

I hate that frigging name!

She chose not to reprimand him for his choice of offensive name. "What is it going to take for you to admit your guilt?"

"I don't know, let me think. Ah yes, I'll admit it when bloody Hell freezes over because, read my lips here, I didn't frigging do what you're trying to pin on me."

"Mr Jordan, I'm going to leave the room for a few minutes. Maybe you'd like to have a word with your client in my absence. Make him aware how foolish his claims are in light of the evidence we've got at our disposal to prove the opposite."

"I think that's a very wise move, Inspector," Jordan replied. He raised a hand to prevent Zappel from objecting.

Carla ended the recording session and she followed Sara out of the room. The uniformed officer who had been overseeing the events left with them. "Can you remain here, Jon?"

"Of course, ma'am."

"Good. I need a quick coffee. Come on, we'll go upstairs, let them stew for ten minutes or so." They walked up the hallway to the sound of Jo Zappel shouting at his solicitor.

"That man sure has a bloody mouth on him. Do you think the solicitor is safe in there with him?" Carla asked.

"Jon's only a few feet away. He'll return to the room if he feels things are getting out of hand in there."

"What do you make of what he's said so far?"

"He's lying. Trying to bloody pull the wool over our eyes, probably because we're both women." Sara reached the top of the stairs and pushed open the door to the incident room. "Coffee?"

"Please," Carla replied. She sank into a nearby chair and heaved out a frustrated sigh.

"Don't let the fucker get to you. We'll have this, let him sweat it out with his brief for a while and then start the interview from the beginning again, if we have to. I'm not going to let the bastard win. We've got all the evidence we need to convict the bastard, anyway."

Carla nodded and took the proffered cup from Sara. "He's going to be a tough one to crack, but as you say, how can he ignore all the evidence which points to him? He can't, not really."

"Yep, it's a matter of us being patient and grinding him down until he admits the truth. We'll give it a few more hours in there and do the same, then leave the room, let him stew and vent his anger on his solicitor and start all over again, if we have to. I refuse to let this bastard win."

"You're made of stronger stuff than I am."

"Sorry to interrupt," Craig began, "I take it things aren't going too well in there then?"

"That's an understatement. Sorry, guys, I wasn't intentionally keeping you out of the loop. So far, the interview hasn't gone according to plan. In spite of all the evidence I've presented him with, he's flat out denying both murders."

Craig scratched his head. "Okay, maybe start off denying it until you can prove otherwise, but then I would've thought he'd have caved in. Is that the way it works?"

"Normally, yes. However, this time, he's being resolute we've got it wrong."

Carla sighed. "And yet, was it my imagination that when we walked into the room he seemed defeated?"

Sara thought back and clicked her fingers. "You're right. Can you pinpoint when his demeanour changed, Carla?"

Her partner blew out a breath and tapped a pen on the desk as she thought. "I could be wrong, but around the time you mentioned the second victim."

Sara contemplated her suggestion. "Maybe, I can't say I noticed, I was too busy trying to pin him down." She sipped at her drink. "The change in MO is a peculiar one. I mean, yes, I know we've dealt with criminals before where they've changed MO to try and get us off the scent, but that's been over a few months. We're talking less than twenty-four hours between the crimes here."

"It does seem strange," Carla admitted. She downed the rest of her coffee.

Sara did the same. "Something we need to consider going forward. All right, we'll get back to it. Maybe the solicitor has managed to work his magic in our absence. We'll soon find out. See you laters!"

Sara and Carla threw their empty cups in the bin as they passed and took a slow and steady trip back downstairs. "How have things been?" Sara asked Jon, still standing guard outside the room.

He lowered his voice to reply, "Things settled down when you left."

"I know I shouldn't ask, but I'm going to anyway. Did you over-hear anything of interest?"

"Sorry, nothing new. He just repeated what he'd been saying to you during the interview."

Sara nodded. "Okay, it was worth a shot. Let's get back to it, folks. I sense a long few hours ahead of us." Sara pinned another smile in place and entered the room. She and Carla sat at the desk while Jon took up his position at the back of the room once more.

Carla set the recorder going and Sara asked, "I hope the break was beneficial and that Mr Jordan has put you on the right path, Jo?"

"He hasn't, so it was a waste of time you leaving the room. I've got nothing further to add to what I've already said."

"I see. Well, I have all the time in the world. My colleague will tell you, I don't have much of a home life and tend to spend most of my spare time at work, so don't think I'll be giving in trying to seek the truth anytime soon. Just warning you."

Carla nodded and said, "It's true. Once the inspector decides to sink her teeth into something, she rarely lets go."

"So fucking what! I couldn't give a shit if you have a decent home life or not, I'm not surprised a bitch like you doesn't have a significant other waiting for you."

"I didn't say that. My husband accepts I'm a professional and that I have exceptional standards to uphold. Oh, where were we? Ah, yes. We left you having a word with Mr Jordan. What was the outcome?" Sara directed her question to the duty solicitor.

"My client is steadfast in his decision that he's done nothing wrong. He has reiterated his innocence time and time again, and yet you're insisting on pushing the issue, Inspector. I have to say, I don't see the object in continually going around in circles."

"Don't you? Even though two women have lost their lives, and we have evidence to back up our claims that your client was involved in both crimes? Shame on you, Mr Jordan."

The solicitor grinned, looked at his notebook and jotted something down.

"Let's start from the beginning, Jo. By the way, your coat and hat are on the way to the lab now; we should have the results back in a few days. Until that time, you'll be remaining in custody. It's up to you how we proceed. My advice would be to tell the truth, it's only going to hamper your future if you continually deny your involvement in the crimes."

"So be it. Because, lady, that's exactly what I fucking intend on doing. You can't pin something on me just because you have the evidence to back it up."

Sara frowned. "Really? How do you work that one out? That's exactly how these things go down. It's up to you to prove your innocence. Denying you were at certain places at a specific time just doesn't cut it." She tapped both crime scene photos. "Especially as we have the evidence to the contrary right here at our disposal. Not just any old evidence, actual solid evidence I'm talking about here.

So, do yourself a favour and tell us why you killed these two women."

"And I've told you several times, too many to mention, that I have done no such thing. Why won't you believe me?"

Sara let out an exasperated sigh. "Because of this... cracking evidence. Some of the best incriminating evidence I've ever held in my hands. I can't understand your logic in denying your involvement any longer. Give us all a break and admit the truth."

"Are you fucking deaf or just plain stupid? I ain't admitting to nothing because I didn't frigging do it. Bloody hell, how many more times do I have to say it? Actually, you know what, don't answer that, because screw you, bitch. From now on only two words are going to leave my lips: no comment."

And that's how the afternoon panned out for all of them. Intense frustration filled the room, both parties stubborn to a fault. But at the end of the day, Jo Zappel stuck to his word and continued to go down the 'no comment' route.

At seven o'clock, Sara decided enough was enough for one day. Zappel was thrown into a cell, still protesting his innocence.

"Pain in the bloody arse, why can't these criminals make life easy for us and damn well confess when we have them by the short and bloody curlies? Boils my piss, I can tell you," Sara complained on the way back up the stairs to the incident room.

"You don't say," Carla mumbled behind her.

The rest of the team had all stayed behind, eager to see what the outcome was to the interview that had taken all afternoon to conduct.

Throwing up her hands in frustration, Sara filled them in. "So, in a nutshell, that's it, folks. We'll get back to it in the morning. At least, we should be able to sleep better in our beds tonight, knowing there's a killer off the streets of Hereford, whether he's willing to admit to the crimes he's committed or not. By the way, that's your cue to pack up for the night."

The team didn't need telling twice. Sara turned to walk into her office and caught the sound of a text going off. *Probably one of the team's partners demanding to know where they are. I'm surprised*

Mark hasn't left me a message. She collected her coat and returned to find Carla staring at her mobile. "Hey, what's up? Nothing's wrong is it?"

Carla waggled her phone. "I'm not sure. It's from Gary."

"Shit! What does he want?"

"To see me."

"And are you going to?" Sara wondered what the tosser wanted after her recent conversation with him, something she'd managed to keep from her partner.

"No way. Not after the way he treated me. I'd have to have a screw loose for that to happen. Are we fit?"

Sara giggled. "Yep, to drop. I don't know about you, but I'm dead on my feet. Any plans for this evening?"

"Straight home, open a tin of soup, sling some bread in the toaster and feet up in front of the TV for a few hours, that is if I can keep my eyes open long enough. I'm cream-crackered."

Sara switched off the lights and they left the building together. "I'm hoping Mark is at home with his pinny on, rustling up something nice to eat. I'm famished."

"It must be nice having someone like Mark to rely on. He never lets you down, does he?"

Sara stopped and faced Carla. "You'll find a decent bloke who treats you right one day, sweetie, don't give up just yet."

"You reckon? They all seem ideal candidates for the role for the first few months and then bang, everything turns upside down and I'm back to square one, being single and dwelling in self-pity mode."

"Hang in there, you're still young. Please, whatever you do, promise me you won't go down the online dating route."

"No fear of that."

"Good. Oh, I forgot to tell you, last night when Mark came home, he told me he'd had a confrontation with one of his customers and ended up with a bloody nose for his trouble."

"What? Who in their right mind attacks an effing vet? Was he all right?"

"Yep, I cleaned him up and tried to pressure him into making a statement against the guy, but he was having none of it."

"Any reason?"

Sara pressed the key fob and her car doors clunked open. "He said it showed how much the guy loved his pet. He was examining a German Shepherd's hips at the time."

"I suppose he's right, but bloody hell, you don't go around beating up the guy who is trying to make your dog better for fuck's sake!"

"I know. He's too soft, I've told him that time and time again."

"He's an absolute gem. You've landed on your feet there, Sara. Goodnight."

She smiled and waved. "See you tomorrow. Chin up."

"I'm fine. Don't worry about me," Carla shouted over her shoulder.

Concerned, Sara sat in the driver's seat and fiddled with this and that, pretending she was looking for something, all the time keeping a close eye on what Carla was doing behind her in her own vehicle. She couldn't tell one way or another judging by her partner's expression. Eventually, Carla pulled up next to her and lowered her window.

"Everything all right?"

"I'm fine. I've lost my shopping list, it's my turn to stock up the cupboards on the way home. Enjoy your evening."

"I will. Hope you find it soon."

Carla drove off and Sara set off soon after. She hated fibbing to her partner, but she had a suspicion Carla would back down and see Gary, despite assuring her that she had no intention of getting in touch with him. *Maybe I should hang around, go and see him. Nope, I need to trust Carla will do the right thing and steer clear of the idiot.*

She slotted into first gear and drove home with *Smooth Radio* on in the background. Mark rang when she was five minutes away from home.

"I was just about to ring you. Are you at home?"

"I am. Dinner's ready, how long will you be?"

She smiled. Carla was right about one thing, Mark was an absolute gem. "Three minutes, give or take. Sorry for postponing our date. I hope there was enough food in the cupboards? What are we having?"

"It's a surprise. See you soon."

She ended the call and rotated her head which clicked several times during its rotation. "I could do with a long, hot soak in a bath. No chance of that happening if dinner is ready."

As she entered the road, she saw Mark standing on the doorstep, holding Misty. He was always there for her—for that, she would be eternally grateful. Not for the first time, she hoped Carla would soon find a love as great as theirs.

*A*fter a surprisingly restful night's sleep, Sara got on the road the following morning and was at the station by eight-forty-five a.m. She breezed through the main door with a cheery smile. "Morning, Jeff. Another beautiful day."

Her smile proved to be infectious because he beamed at her and bowed his head. "And a very good morning to you, ma'am."

"How was our guest overnight?"

"The night staff reported that all was quiet in that department, you'll be pleased to know."

"Good, good. Let me get a double dose of coffee going through my veins and then Carla and I will come down for round two."

"Sounds like a good plan. He's been fed and watered. Would you believe he chose porridge for breakfast?"

They both laughed. "Starting as he means to go on, eh? I bet ours tastes better than the one they serve in prison."

"Maybe that was his intention. To see what the difference was at each establishment."

Sara sniggered. "We mustn't mock. Slapped wrists for both of us."

Carla came through the main entrance. "Morning, anything wrong?"

Sara inclined her head. "Everything is just perfect here, what about you?"

Her partner shot Jeff an uncomfortable look and punched in the number to open the security door without responding. Sara knew then that something was amiss. She followed Carla through the door, and Jeff raised a questioning eyebrow in her wake.

"Carla, don't walk off, tell me what's going on," Sara shouted, trying her hardest to keep up with her.

"I'm fine. Keen to get to my desk and get on with the day ahead."

"Why don't I believe you?"

"I don't know. Maybe you should trust me now and again."

"Ouch! That was uncalled for. Stop, look me in the eye and swear to me that you're okay." Carla's pace slowed ahead of her, but she refused to face Sara. She caught up and touched Carla's arm hard enough to make her turn her way. "Carla?"

Tears formed in her eyes, but thankfully remained just there. So much for her day starting out well.

"I'm sorry. I promised myself that I wouldn't break down in front of you. I'm doing my utmost to adhere to that."

"Need a conflab in the ladies'?"

Carla smiled. "Not this time. It would be great if you would just allow me to get on with my work today. I'll get back to you if I need to chat, okay? And no, that's not me shutting you out. It's about saving myself from letting the emotions take over when all I'm trying to do is keep them at bay. Is that okay with you?"

"Of course. You know what I say about dealing with an emotional state, don't you?"

Carla wiped her eyes with the cuff of her jacket and frowned. "No, what's that?"

"I tend to put it aside until mid-morning, giving the caffeine enough time to work its magic."

Chuckling, Carla shook her head. "Where would you be without your caffeine?"

Sara gasped. "Don't, I dread to think. What if some insect came along and wiped out the coffee trees overnight? Can you imagine what state the economy would be in, dealing with people with withdrawal issues?"

"One problem there, I don't think coffee grows on trees. Maybe you're not the aficionado you make out to be."

Sara pulled a face. "It's bushes or shrubs actually. Anyway, I was testing you, to see if you were awake and with it before we get to work on Zappel."

Carla raised an eyebrow. "Yeah, right. What time do you want to start on him?"

"I'm in no rush. He's had breakfast, let him sit and ponder his mistakes for a little while longer. Giving me enough time to sort through the post while downing two cups of coffee. And it doesn't grow on trees, eh? You live and learn every bloody day, don't you?"

Sara played along, glad to see her partner's face crack. *My job is done.*

After tending to her regular mind-numbing chores and downing the obligatory cups of coffee to ensure her day got off to a good start, Sara returned to the incident room to collect Carla.

"We're going in for round two, guys. Keep digging, we're going to need to lay our hands on every last bit of evidence we can find to nail him to the wall."

"I would have thought we'd have provided you with enough already," Will muttered.

"While I don't disagree with you, Will, it's always good to keep at it, trying to find more."

"You can count on us, boss. If the evidence is out there, we'll get our hands on it," Craig chipped in.

"I don't doubt it for a second. Carla, are you ready for this?"

"More than ready. I wonder what kind of welcome he'll be offering us this morning."

"There's only one way to find out. I've already contacted Jeff, he's getting him moved to the interview room and the duty solicitor has just arrived. Another reason I needed to delay the interview this morning."

"Ah, okay. So it wasn't you trying to work out if I was right or not about the coffee element?" Carla sniggered and left the room.

She chased after her and caught up at the top of the stairs. "Cheeky mare, and no, I haven't been sitting on my arse, trawling through the internet either, in a quest to see if you were correct."

"I believe you," Carla shouted. She raced down the stairs and smiled up at Sara once she reached the bottom.

"Don't think you've heard the last of this particular topic, Miss Jameson."

"I'm dying to hear your reaction when you learn the truth."

Sara glared at her through narrowed eyes. "It can wait." They walked the length of the corridor side by side and Sara paused with her hand on the doorknob to suck in a few calming breaths before she entered the room.

"You've got this, Sara." Carla winked at her.

"Let's hope so."

Jo Zappel and his solicitor were already at the table. Neither of them turned when Sara and Carla entered the room. Sara set the file of evidence before her and sat down opposite the two men. "Good morning to both of you. Another fine day." She smiled at the uniformed officer standing along the far wall.

"It is," Mr Jordan agreed, staring at his pad. He glanced up and smiled. "My client has something to say."

Sara raised a finger. "Let's get the recording underway first, shall we? DS Jameson, if you'd do the honours?"

Carla set the recorder going, announced who was present in the room and then handed the proceedings over to Sara. "Mr Jordan, am I to understand your client wishes to tell us something after his stint in a cell overnight?"

"He does. While he admits he was present at the first crime scene, he is adamant he knows nothing about the second crime."

Sara glanced at Carla and frowned. She turned back to Jordan and said, "I'm confused. He says he was present at Val Purcell's home on the night she was killed, is that correct?" Her gaze drifted over to the suspect. His head was bowed and he was staring at the table.

"That's an affirmative."

Sara shook her head. "I'm sorry, but I find that extremely hard to believe. We have the evidence placing him at the second crime scene. You've seen that evidence for yourself and yet, it would appear to me that you haven't given your client any guidance in accepting his guilt."

"Did you not hear me, Inspector? He's adamant he wasn't involved in the second crime."

"I heard you, I just find it very hard to fathom when all the evidence tells us the opposite is true."

Zappel's head rose, and Sara saw the tears in his eyes. There was no form of emotion tugging at her heartstrings, she'd been down this road before with many other criminals seeking sympathy. "I didn't do it. I swear I didn't." His voice faltered on the words.

Carla nudged Sara under the table. She nudged her partner in return and then queried, "Then who did? You told us yesterday that no one else has access to your vehicle and yet, your vehicle was involved in the crime. You can see that for yourself, so you'll forgive any confusion on my part, won't you?"

"That's right. I don't know how someone got their hands on my car without me knowing. I'm not trying to deceive you here."

"You're not? Then explain to me how your vehicle was seen close to the crime and you were caught on CCTV cameras getting into that vehicle. You admitted the man in the photo was wearing your coat and hat, I believe."

"I didn't admit anything of the sort. Stop trying to trick me. I'm doing my best here to help you out."

"And I appreciate the efforts you are making to help us get to the truth, I truly do. But things just aren't adding up, I need to find out why. You can understand that, can't you?"

His head lowered again and he shuffled in his chair. "I'm not sure I'm ever going to be able to convince you of my innocence. Therefore, you need to do what you need to do. I'm sick to death of being grilled and being called a damn liar. I've done my best to tell you the truth, and I have to say, it hasn't got me very far, has it?"

His words touched a nerve in Sara. She studied the man's down-hearted demeanour for a while before she sat back and said, "Let's go over things one more time, to ensure we haven't missed anything out, then you can have your wish and I'll call an end to the interview."

Zappel groaned but nodded all the same. "If you insist."

"Val Purcell, the first victim, what happened there?"

"I knocked on the door, intending to scam some money out of her. Told her there was a dodgy tile on her roof."

"So why kill her?"

"I didn't." He sighed.

"Then who did? Are you telling me someone else was with you at the house?"

His silence and refusal to answer the question lay heavy in the air. "Mr Zappel, I've been at this more years than I care to remember. I have developed this uncanny knack of knowing when someone isn't telling me the truth." He opened his mouth to speak, but she silenced him with her raised hand. "Or if that person is avoiding something. Tell me I'm wrong, if you can?"

His gaze bore into hers for a few moments and then drifted off to the side of the room. "Are we done here? I'm getting bored with going over the same questions all the time."

"We'll be done when I clarify something important and not before. You are going to be charged with both murders..." He blustered his objection, opening and closing his mouth several times. Sara continued, "With the evidence we have to hand, condemning your actions, it's a no-brainer for us. You can object all you like; as I've said before, if you admit you were responsible for both crimes, the court will be more lenient with your sentencing."

"This is utter bullshit." Zappel faced his solicitor. "Don't just sit there and take this from her, do something. Get me out of this mess. Do your frigging job, arsehole!"

Jordan's eyebrow shot up. "Arsehole, am I? Right, I'm out of here. Inspector, do what you will with my *former* client. For the recording, this is me resigning and leaving the room."

Zappel was incensed. "You can't. I won't allow you to run out on me. Come back here, you friggin' moron."

The slamming of the door behind Jordan silenced Zappel.

Sara smiled. "It's not your day today, is it, Jo? You will be placed under arrest for both murders and transferred to a remand centre this afternoon. Dan, can you escort Mr Zappel back to his cell? Thank you."

The young uniformed officer grabbed the struggling Zappel by his cuffed hands and marched him out of the room.

Carla ended the recording and, together, they both let out a long sigh. "That was tough. Do you believe him?" Carla asked.

Sara gathered the file and left her chair. "No chance. He's as guilty as fucking Saddam Hussein was all those years ago."

Shuddering, Carla replied, "I can think of better comparisons. That man gave me the creeps every time his face appeared on the TV."

"Sorry. Yep, me too. Vile, controlling individual. The world is a better place without him."

They trudged back upstairs, Sara deep in thought about what Zappel had said. *Something is off, is he guilty or not?* Once they'd arrived at the incident room, she brought the whiteboard up to date and stared at it for a while. She turned to see the rest of her team silent, all watching her. "Okay, I was mulling things over there for a moment. Here's where we stand. We've arrested Zappel for both murders, except, for some unknown reason—don't bloody ask me why—I believe him when he says he wasn't involved in the second crime. There, I can't believe those words left my mouth either, before you challenge me on that. Carla, what do you think?"

"Possibly. The only thing making a mockery of the situation is the firm evidence we have. The CCTV footage of his car and a person dressed in his coat and hat close to the second murder scene. That's pretty damning evidence to dismiss."

Sara swept a few loose hairs behind her ear. "I know. Believe me, I'd rather be pointing the finger at him, but what if we're wrong? What if that's not the end of the murders even though we have him in custody?"

"If you think that, then why did you arrest him for both?" Carla contested.

Sara shrugged. "Because of the damn evidence. That has to count somewhere along the line, doesn't it?"

"I suppose. What now? We tie all this up and set it aside for the time being?"

Sara sighed. "If only. I think we need to go over everything a few more times just to ensure we're not missing anything vital."

"Like arresting the right suspect?" Carla grumbled.

Sara cocked an eyebrow. "Let's just say, I'd rather arrest him than let him walk the streets. He's guilty as sin for the first murder, so I don't feel like I'm stitching him up. Plus, at the risk of repeating myself, the evidence will back me up when the case goes to court. Damn this bloody gut feeling, sometimes it can be a sodding curse. Just to satisfy my curiosity, we need to carry out a thorough background check on Zappel. Where he works, who he lives with. I know we've seen inside his house; to me, I think he lives alone, but I've been known to be wrong in the past. Does he have a family? Is or was he married? Let's get busy, guys. I'll be in my office chasing up Lorraine and Forensics. Any questions?" The team all shook their heads. "Let's get to work then, dig deep, guys, I know you won't let me down."

She left the incident room and entered her office via the vending machine. On her way to the desk, she paused to look out of the window at the amazing view of the Brecon Beacons, except today, the view reflected her mood. Cloudy and dreary.

Have I done the right thing? Could this come back and bite me in the arse? Sometimes, I have to go with the evidence that's placed before me, don't I? Even so, it's a risky strategy to have to take. Zappel was adamant he had nothing to do with that second crime, to the point of being horrified by the suggestion he would or could rape someone. How does one person go from killing an old woman for her cash to killing a young woman, even raping her before taking her life? None of this makes any sense. If it wasn't for the conclusive evidence we've sourced, I would never link the crimes, not in a million years!

She sat behind her desk and rang Lorraine. "Hi, it's me, Sara. I suppose it's too soon to have any news for me, right?"

"Hi, yes, it is. I'm still working on both victims. What's up? You sound harassed."

"Kind of. We've arrested someone for both crimes. He's admitted he was present at the first murder, denies doing the deed." She let out a sigh. "But we have footage of him obtaining money from the victim's bank with her card."

"Okay, and?"

"And, I've arrested him for the second murder, but…"

"What? You're unsure whether he's the culprit or not? Is that a wise route to take, Sara?"

"Hear me out. Again, we have him as close as damn it to the second scene. CCTV footage of his car, the suspect leaving the alley and returning to his vehicle."

"I see. Then I don't understand what the problem is." Lorraine yawned.

Sara felt sorry for her being on call all hours of the day. "The problem is, my damn gut instinct is telling me something is gravely wrong."

"How is that possible if you have the proof with the footage?"

Sara unwrapped a piece of chewing gum and started masticating it. "Correction, sorry, I should have been clearer. We have a person wearing a coat and hat who looks like the suspect. We haven't actually got a visual of him other than that." She replayed the image in her mind.

"Ah, I can see why this is bugging you, then. It's not cut and dried and that's how you like things, isn't it?"

"Don't you? I'm not really one for banging up the wrong person. I've never done it before and I don't want this to be my first exploit in that direction."

"I get that. Which is where I come into it, right?"

"Yep. Tell me the suspect left semen at the crime scene."

"I can't. Looks like he used a condom."

Sara flung the pen she was using across the room, and it hit the door. "Fuck, not what I wanted to hear."

"I know, I'm sorry. Other than that, there's really nothing more I can offer you."

"Okay, it was worth a shot. I'll be eagerly awaiting your reports on both victims. I'll get in touch with Forensics, see what they have to offer."

"Good luck. Last I heard, they had nothing at all."

"Jesus, can my day get any worse?"

"I doubt it. Sorry, Sara. PMA, love."

"Thanks, speak soon."

She ended the call and bounced back and forth in her chair a few times, after which her frustrations dwindled enough for her to get on and deal with the day's post.

*S*ara rejoined the team at around twelve-thirty. Carla was organising a sandwich run that Craig had volunteered to do. "I was coming to see you, what would you like for lunch?"

"I haven't really thought about it. Egg and cress for a change, on either brown or wholemeal, thanks. Hang on, I'll get my purse."

"No, you won't. I'll get it this time, for a change."

"Thanks, Carla." Sara perched on the desk next to her and watched Carla jot down the rest of the orders and hand the note to Craig. He left the room soon after. "Right, now that's out of the way, where are we?"

Christine started off the proceedings. "I checked for a spouse and come up blank. I then checked for any births, just in case Jo Zappel was living with someone and didn't tie the knot." She checked her notes and looked up again. "I came up with a son, Adam Zappel. The mother was a Daphne Wyatt. I then tried to trace the son and Daphne. The mother died two years ago of breast cancer. But I'm still trying to locate the son."

"Excellent, I take it they lived in the area."

"No. Up north in Morecambe Bay."

"Hmm… okay. Let's try to find out where the son is located now. Good work, Christine."

"Just doing my job, boss."

Sara smiled. "I know. But a bit of praise here and there does wonders, in my opinion. Anyone got anything else?"

"No, nothing yet. It's a bit early for that," Carla said, an edge to her tone.

"The sooner we piece everything together, the quicker we can close down the investigation."

"I know how it works," Carla snapped.

Sara frowned. It was unlike her partner to bite back without reason. "Something wrong, Carla?"

"No, sorry. Things on my mind, that's all."

Sara knew exactly who she was referring to. *Bloody Gary! Even when they're not together, he's causing sodding trouble.* "If you need to unburden yourself, you know where my office is."

"I do. I'm fine."

The rest of the afternoon was spent dipping in and out of her office and geeing up the team with their research duties. At six, Sara announced it was time to leave. "You've done a sterling job today, guys. Thank you for all your efforts. The desk sergeant contacted me half an hour ago to tell me that Zappel was on his way to the remand centre, one less task to worry about. Let's hope the folks of Hereford can sleep well in their beds tonight. I know I'm ready for mine, it's been a mentally tiring day. Go home and get some rest." The team all nodded their agreement and set about switching off their equipment for the night.

Sara dipped back into her office to retrieve her handbag and coat. Carla was the only team member left when she returned. "How's it diddling?"

"I'm fine. You worry too much."

"I hate seeing you so down. It's not like you to snap at me, especially in front of the others like that."

Carla shrugged and rolled her eyes. "Gosh, make me feel worse, why don't you?"

"That wasn't my intention and you know it."

"I know. Sorry."

"I don't want your apologies, all I want is my chilled-out partner back." Sara rubbed Carla's arm, worried about her mental state. Gary had a lot to answer for.

"I'll get there. Once Gary gets the message to leave me alone."

"There's an easy answer to that, block his number on your phone."

"It's not that... it won't stop my head being screwed up, will it?"

Sara cringed. "Screwed up? Don't tell me you still have feelings for him, Carla?"

"I don't know. Sometimes, I hate the fucker for the way he treated me, but the next day..."

"The next day?"

"I think I can't live without him." She finally muttered the admission Sara feared was coming.

Jesus! If only you knew! He didn't admit it, but there's every possibility he was behind you getting beaten up. I can't tell you that though, or should I? Sara toyed with the idea a few seconds longer and then shook her head.

"You need to take time out and weigh up your options. For what it's worth, I think it would be wrong of you to let him back into your life."

"That's easy for you to say, but you don't know what it was like when we were alone together."

"Granted. I can only go by what you've told me about your relationship. You're guilty of remembering the good times and forgetting all the times that were bad. It's what people tend to do when a relationship goes sour."

Carla pouted and snapped, "Don't speak to me as if I'm a child, I'm not."

"I wasn't aware I was. I'm taking a step back and assessing things for what they are. Okay, I have a home to go to. Think about what I've said. What's he asking from you, Carla?"

"I don't know what he wants, except to see me."

"Then it's up to you whether you fall for that one or not. You have to ask yourself why he wants to see you."

Carla stamped her foot in annoyance. "How the bloody hell will I know that unless I meet up with him?"

Sara shrugged. "That's up to you. I'm backing away now. I get the sense that you've already stopped listening to me. The last thing I want to do is fall out with you over Gary. You have to do what's right for you, hon."

"But you forgot to say, 'I won't be there to pick up the pieces if things go pear-shaped', right?"

Sara issued a stiff smile. "That about sums it up."

Knowing what I know about Gary, no, I can't agree to that. Does that make me a bad person? Maybe. Such an awful dilemma.

"Wow, okay, at least I know where I stand."

Sara was torn between telling Carla what she knew and letting her make her own decisions in life, without interference.

Is it my place to tell her what's right and wrong? She's a grown fucking woman for God's sake. But then, could I live with the consequences if things go belly-up?

"Sorry, Carla. You have to put yourself in my shoes, I'm damned if I advise you one way or the other. The only advice I can offer you is to take stock of the last six months, the time you were together, and don't let your heart rule your head. That's me officially butting out now, okay?"

Carla nodded and marched out of the incident room. "Carla, Carla, come back." By the time she reached the top of the stairs, her partner was gone.

"Are you off for the day?"

Sara clutched her chest and spun around. "Jesus, you scared the crap out of me, boss."

"Sorry. I thought you heard me approaching you."

"I didn't, guilty of being in a world of my own."

Carol Price cocked her head to the side. "Now you mention it, you seem a bit stressed. I have five minutes if you need to bend my ear about something."

"I'm fine. Things will work out good in the end, I'm sure."

"Glad to hear it. Fancy a drink?"

"Ugh... I promised myself an early day, I got home late last night after interviewing the suspect."

"Ah, yes, so I heard. I was hoping you'd drop by and give me an update. I don't appreciate hearing about things second hand, Inspector."

"Damn. I forgot. It wasn't intentional, I can assure you."

"Did I say it was? I'm aware of the pressure you and your team are under. I'll let you off this time."

"Thanks, boss. The suspect was arrested and is tucked up safely in the remand centre now."

"I know. Jeff informed me as I came into the station earlier. I'd been to a meeting with Social Services. No, you don't want to know what that was about. More paperwork for me to file and directives to get signed off for a memo heading your way in the near future."

Groaning, Sara started to descend the stairs and the chief caught her up. "I've had enough shop talk for the day."

"Are you sure everything is all right, Sara?"

"Yes, boss. Ignore me. I'm grouchy and in dire need of a glass of wine and cuddle with my hubby."

"Ah, I was going to suggest I can supply the wine, but a cuddle is another matter entirely."

Sara turned and offered her boss a smile. "You're a good woman, DCI Price."

"I know. Even though I have several people around me who would eagerly stab me in the back given the opportunity."

Sara gasped. "Hey, I hope you don't consider me one of them."

"No, I don't. Although saying that, due to the extra pressure I've put you under lately, concerning the cuts, I've seen the anger in your eyes at times."

Sara paused and opened her mouth to object. The chief carried on walking. "But..."

"No buts. I totally understand the untenable position I've put you in. Enough said about that, we've covered that particular topic more times than I care to remember."

"Okay. I haven't got the head to fight our corner again, not right now anyway."

"Good. I'm glad we agree about something."

They reached the main door, bid Jeff farewell for the evening and separated in the car park. Sara felt relieved the chief hadn't insisted on taking her for the drink she'd suggested. She got in the car and rang Mark. "Hey, I'm on my way. Are you at home yet?"

"Yep, dinner is on the go."

"Aww… I was going to stop off at the supermarket and treat us to a nice steak."

"Great minds. Already sorted."

"Okay, a bottle of wine perhaps to go with it?"

"Done, just come home."

"Yes, sir. Can't wait to see you. It's been a long day."

"I'll give you a foot massage later, to help you relax, if you like?"

"Sounds wonderful. I'm up for that. I'll be fifteen minutes."

She ended the call and sat back to mull over her conversation with Carla. *Have I done the right thing, keeping the secret from her? My heart says yes but my head is saying no. Bugger, what should I do? What about the investigation? Is my gut feeling right about Jo Zappel, or has it gone to pot?* She shook her head to dislodge the dilemmas rattling around and decided to ring her mother instead. "Hi, Mum, how are you both?"

"Sara, is that you?"

She smiled. "Yes, Mum, it's me. I know it's been a few weeks since I've been in touch, don't make me feel guilty."

"I wasn't having a go, dear. I was just surprised to hear from you. How are you?"

"Tired. It's been a long week so far. What about you and Dad coming over to us for Sunday lunch this week?"

"Oh my, that would be lovely. Are you sure it's not too much of an inconvenience after you having a long week?"

"Not at all. Mark and I will share the cooking as usual. Come to us at around twelve, we'll have a good old natter while we're preparing the dinner. Anything in particular you fancy?"

"Just someone cooking a meal for me for a change would make my day, darling. You choose, we'll be grateful for anything you put in front of us."

"Leave it with us. We'll see you, then. Love you, Mum. Send Dad my love, won't you?"

"Of course I will. Thank you for thinking of us, sweetheart."

Sara ended the call and turned up the radio to enjoy the rest of the drive home.

8

*A*dam had watched from afar when the coppers had taken his father away. Panic had set in and forced him into hiding. He was sure his dad would drop him in it with the police, so he'd made the conscious decision not to go back to the house, just in case they came to arrest him. He glanced around at the squat he was taking temporary refuge in and shuddered. This type of life wasn't for him, although it would have to do for now. He'd learnt about this place from a friend of his; Wayne was down on his luck, but Adam hadn't known that when he'd got in touch, seeking help.

He had itchy feet, needed to get out of this dosshouse, but where else could he go? This area was relatively new to him and without his father being on hand, he didn't have a clue where to go or what to do for the best.

Had the police arrested him? How did they know where to find him? What about his car, had it been impounded? He had dozens of legitimate questions rattling around in his head and no sign of any clear answers.

He decided to get out of this dump and go for a few beers while he contemplated what to do next with his life, now that his lifeline had been cut off. He left the squat and strolled into the Traveller's Rest public house on the corner of the next street. There were enough customers in there for him not to stick out in the crowd. He ordered a pint of bitter and sat at the bar, people-watching. Several men were knocking their drinks back as if it was the last beer they were ever likely to taste. Maybe the pandemic had caused their anxiety or maybe it had always been there to start with.

Observing the other customers, he gulped large mouthfuls of his drink and mulled over what to do next.

Where can I go? Not back to the house with the cops crawling all over it. Have I left any possessions behind? They're sure to get a warrant to search the property. Damn, this wasn't in the plan at all. Why did I screw up? His mind dwelled on the last point as the image of the second victim drifted into it. He grinned, remembering her squirming beneath him as he took advantage of her slender body. *Good job I used a rubber. No chance of them pinning that one on me. Maybe the old man will admit to both crimes, he'd better! I won't be pleased if he doesn't.* Relief had flooded through him when the police had come to arrest the wrong guy.

Things had turned rowdy in the corner. There was a card game going on, no money involved from what he could see, but that might have been for the landlord's sake. He watched for the next five minutes as the situation escalated, until the landlord had to step in and ask the drunk, who appeared to be causing all the problems, to leave.

"Come on, Bob, what have I told you about starting trouble in here? I won't have it. I run a peaceful gaff, where people come for a drink, knowing they will be safe. It would be better for all concerned if you went on your way, without any fuss." The landlord had muscles the size of Popeye's.

Bob stared up at him, and he seemed confused by what was going on, to begin with, until his shoulders relaxed and he admitted defeat.

Something sparked in Adam's mind. He glanced on, intrigued by how things would play out. He got to the bottom of his glass and didn't bother ordering another pint. His interest in what was taking place on the other side of the room was drawing him like a magnet.

He left his bar stool and tottered a little. *Shit, how many have I had?* The drunk began tussling with the landlord, objecting to being manhandled and refusing to leave the pub. Adam had an inkling as to what was about to happen and pre-empted it. He left through the side door and waited out in the car park, hiding in the shadows of the large oak tree at the edge close to the exit.

The door to the pub flew open. The landlord chucked poor Bob out on his arse.

"'Ere, you cawn't tweat me like that! I'wl get the copsss on you," Bob shouted from his cold spot on the tarmac. The man remained seated for the next few minutes as if gathering the willpower to attempt to get to his feet. He turned over onto his hands and knees and paused, likely trying to figure out how to proceed next. Defeated, he slumped back onto his bum and slowly rotated his head around the car park.

"Will someone please 'elp me?"

Adam waited it out for a little while longer, until the man faced the other way and then he emerged from the shadows, whistling a merry tune. "Hello, there. What's all this? Been kicked out, have you?"

"Yes. Can ye get me up? Me legss won't work."

Adam helped the drunk to his feet. It was a genuine effort, he wasn't the strongest of men and the drunk was a dead weight, not willing to assist him at all. "Jesus, will you at least try to help me, moron?"

"'Ere you cawn't call me dat. Get away from me, I down't need ye 'elp."

"I'm here now. Come on, give me a break and at least put your legs underneath you, ready for them to take your weight; they're no good being stretched out like that, are they?"

"I'm dowing me best."

"Right, this is your final warning. One last try, if you're not willing to help, I'm gonna leave you here. Got that?"

"Yeah, got it."

With the drunk's minimal assistance, Adam managed to right him onto his feet. "Gotcha, now where's your car?"

"I ain't got one. Cawn't afford one."

"Great. Where do you live?"

"A few roads that way." The drunk pointed over to the left.

"Okay, let's see if we can get you home in one piece."

"Aww... you're a gwood man."

Adam slung the man's arm around his neck and followed the drunk's instructions on which direction to take. They got there eventually, through more of Adam's effort than the drunk's. He deposited the man on his doorstep, propped him up against the wall and rang the bell, then he bolted. He ducked down the alley at the side of the house and listened.

"What the fuck! Are you bloody drunk again? Get in here, you utter twatface. I should have carried out my threat to leave you years ago. All you do is make my life a fucking misery. Look at the frigging money you're spending to get in this state. I could be sunning myself in Marbella with the amount you waste on booze every damn month. I've had it with you. From Monday, you start putting your wages into my bank account. I'll dish out pocket money every week, if that's what it takes." The angry woman sighed. "Get in here. Look at you, you haven't got it in you to even walk straight. What the actual fuck! You know what? Scratch what I just said; first thing Monday morning, I'm ringing a bloody solicitor about a divorce and if you think you're going to get your hands on this house, you've got another think coming."

"But, Nancy... I wove you. Give me one more twy. I prowise I'wl change."

"Do you know how many bloody times I've heard that empty promise over the years? Thousands. I've had it with you. I need a man who can care for me, not piss all his hard-earned money up the frigging wall. Jesus, what's that smell? Have you pissed yourself? You disgust me."

Adam snuck a peek around the wall to see the woman get behind Bob the drunk and shove him through the front door, slapping him around the head at the same time.

"Once too often. Now you're going to pay for letting me and the kids down. Jesus, get up to bed before they see the frigging state you're in. You make me sick. Selfish, brainless fucking sod. It's all about your needs, isn't it? Always has been and always will be. Those kids up there need new shoes for school and there's you, spending money we haven't got down the bloody pub. I've had it, you hear me? Had it!"

The door slammed behind the couple and Adam let out a laugh. *Bloody glad I ain't married if that's the consequences of having a few bevvies down at the local.* He tried to put his own life back on course, after doing his good deed for the day, delivering the drunk home. Had he had the use of a car, Adam would have nicked it, but something about the state the man was in had touched a nerve with him.

There was movement halfway up the street, headlights entered the road and a car stopped. He emerged and walked towards the vehicle. It was pitch black, only a couple of streetlights working at the far end. Perfect for what he had in mind. His pace quickened.

The man got out of his car and locked it. He was holding a brief-case and paused to put his keys away in his jacket, then began searching for something else. Adam took his chance. He withdrew the knife he had tucked into the waistband of his trousers and plunged it into the man's back, several times. He fell to the ground immediately. Adam rummaged through the man's jacket pocket and removed the car keys.

Behind him, a woman screamed. He looked back and saw the woman leave the house and run down the small flight of steps that lead up to the front door.

"Mike, Mike, are you all right? Come back here, you! Help, someone please help me. He's stealing our car. Someone call the police and an ambulance."

Adam jumped into the car and drove off before the woman could get close enough to identify him. *Shit! That's not how I expected it to go down. I didn't get the chance to finish the fucker off. What if he got a good look at me?* His hands shook and he kept looking in the rear-view mirror until he turned the next corner. *Jesus, now I'll have to get to him at the hospital. Why do I always cock things up? Dad, where are you when I need you the most?*

On his way to prison, that's where he is. I'm going to do all I can to make sure I don't end up in the cell next to him. I need to get away, as far away from here as possible. But where do I go? Not knowing this damn area will be tricky, won't it?

He couldn't leave, not until he'd finished the bloke off. Reaching over, he searched the glove compartment for a possible name and found what he was looking for: the car's log book. Who in their right mind kept that kind of documentation in their car? This genius, obviously. He slammed the glove compartment shut again and drove in the direction of the hospital.

He would sit and wait for the ambulance to arrive and then strike again, if necessary. Hopefully, the guy won't make it, which will save him the job of taking care of any loose ends.

Adam grew tired, it had been a hectic couple of days. He rested his head back and his eyes drooped until he heard a couple of giggling young women pass the car. Alert mode took over.

His attention was drawn to the petite blonde wearing a nurse's uniform. He watched the pair until they parted. The brunette got in a car, and she shouted to the other woman, offering her a lift for a final time, but the blonde said she could do with the walk to clear her head.

He started up the engine and crawled along behind the woman. She had a determined stride going on. She upped her pace as she entered the main street. He decided to put his foot down, go past her. Adam studied her in his wing mirror as he passed and then circled back at the end of the road instead of turning right with the flow of traffic.

He drove down a side road and again pulled onto the main street, his heart skipping several beats. *Where is she? Shit! She was there one minute and gone the next.*

Slamming his fists onto the steering wheel, he pressed hard on the accelerator and peered into every road he drove past. There she was, down the second one. He chose to drive through the next available street, hoping it would lead to the one she was walking down. To his relief, it did. Before long, he was crawling along behind her again. The road grew narrower; he peered up ahead, there was a 'no entry' sign blocking his path.

It was now or never.

He parked the car, leapt out of the vehicle and casually approached her. She eyed him with caution and stepped to the edge of the pavement to give him room to pass.

His erection stood to attention and was on the verge of becoming painful. Doubling back, he hooked an arm around her neck, and cupped his other hand over her mouth, preventing her from screaming. She stomped on his foot and kicked out at his shins, catching him once or twice on the bony part. "You fucking bitch. You'll pay for that."

She mumbled something under his palm and then tried to bite him. He was quick to respond and slammed an elbow in her face. She cried out beneath his hand.

"Fighting the inevitable is only going to make things worse. Give in to it and I might even keep you alive at the end of it."

She bit his palm again, and this time her teeth connected properly and did some damage. Adam yelled out and watched the blood trickle from his hand onto the woman's uniform.

"Jesus, you fucking whore."

He pounded her with his fists until she was lying on the ground, gasping for breath. They both were. She sobbed and pleaded with him to let her go.

"No chance, not until I've had what's under that uniform."

She wriggled beneath him as he undid the zip to his trousers. "No, please. I don't want this."

"No, but I do, and I have every intention of winning this game. Keep still and I'll set you free afterwards. I know where you live. If you fight me, I'm going to come after your flatmate." He took a punt that she was single, sharing a house or flat with another woman, knowing how far a nurse's salary would likely get her.

Her wriggling ceased.

He got to work.

She lay there motionless, staring up at the night sky. He did the deed, then reached into the back of his trousers and pulled out the ten-inch blade he favoured. Adam pressed his hand down harder over her mouth. She tried to cry out, her eyes clouded with fear as the knife rose above his head and then pierced her chest.

Not once, twice or three times, but four.

The best part was yet to come.

He watched on and saw the light fade from her eyes, and then her struggling beneath him became a thing of the past.

He zipped up his trousers and jumped to his feet. Once he realised he hadn't used a condom this time, he kicked out at her body. *Shit! She proved to be too tempting, I slipped up.* He removed his jacket and used it to wipe out her vagina. His frustration and anxiety grew at the thought of getting caught, so he rubbed harder to get rid of any possible DNA. Then he ran back to the car and drove off. He stopped a few streets away and dumped his jacket in one of the bins at the back of a small shop. *Maybe I should have burned her damn body instead.* He shrugged and turned on the stereo.

Taking a life meant nothing, as long as it worked out well for him.

Now he was mobile again, and the world was his oyster, except it wasn't, not right now. He had one more task to do before he could leave town and start over somewhere new. He'd only shown up in this dump to be close to his father after he'd deserted him all those years ago. Now, he was no longer going to be around, so why remain in Hereford? A dump of a so-called city. *Ha! Just because it has a cathedral. It's a bloody dive other than that.*

He arrived back at the spot where he'd managed to park the car earlier, before he was distracted and his other needs had taken over. Exhausted by his efforts from pinning the nurse down, his eyes drooped. *I'll catch forty winks while I can.* He drifted off, and the crimes he'd committed in the past three days surfaced and played havoc with his mind. But the image that was prominent in his dreams was the one of his father being taken away by the police. Maybe he should have helped him in some way. But four coppers had shown up, what could he have done to stop them from taking him? Nothing!

Stirring from his restless dozing, he wiped the sleep out of his eyes. A siren sounded in the distance. Is this the one he'd been waiting for? Of course, there was every chance the ambulance had already deposited the man at the hospital while he was indisposed following the damn nurse. He hadn't thought about that before he had fallen asleep. He had the man's name, why hadn't he gone inside to check with reception if he'd arrived or not? His head was a mess. *I'm losing it! Father, you've done this to me. You have always been a waste of space over the years. You're still making me mess up now!*

The ambulance arrived, and he released a relieved sigh when the woman who had chased after him got out of the back of it. He settled down in the car and waited. Sensing he could be in for a long wait if the wife was going to be sitting beside her husband all the time.

Maybe he'd have to kill her as well.

9

Sara received the call from the control centre around five that morning. With sore eyes needing matchsticks to keep them open, she drove to the scene of the crime.

Carla was already there, talking to Lorraine, when she pulled up alongside them.

"Let me tog up and I'll be with you shortly." She fetched a new protective suit and shoe covers from the boot and slipped into them.

The morning was frosty and chilled her to the bone, especially after leaving her warm bed so early. "Blimey, it's cold enough to freeze your tits off this morning. Not what I was expecting at this time of year. Anyway, that's my morning moan out of the way. What have we got, Lorraine?"

"Good morning to you, too. You should have been here when I first showed up, a couple of hours ago, it was a lot colder then. Bloody climate change, fancy having to contend with freezing overnight temperatures in May. Anyhoo! Getting back to the poor victim. We have a young female nurse. Raped and stabbed."

"Shit! I need to ask the most obvious question, any DNA left at the scene?" She gave Lorraine a hopeful smile.

Lorraine winked. "There just might be a soupçon left in the vagina, by the look of things. I'll know more when I get her back to the lab."

"Good news at last. I don't suppose there were any witnesses." Sara glanced up and down the road that narrowed a few feet ahead of her. There were houses at the top of the street and a line of garages in front of them.

"None that were hanging around waiting to speak to us; of course, that doesn't mean there weren't any. Maybe the woman screamed, perhaps someone heard her and chose to ignore it."

"Possibly. Who called it in?"

"A woman who was on her way to fetch her car to go to work. She lives at the house on the corner of the next road. She was severely traumatised when I got here, so I sent her home. Lizzie Martin is her name."

Sara peered over her shoulder. "Which house? Can you point to it?"

"The one with the blue door."

"Thanks, we'll go and speak to her soon. Can you tell me anything else about the victim?"

"Bruising is developing on her face, across her mouth. I suspect she was grabbed violently from behind by her killer, forced to the ground, subjected to her heinous ordeal and then stabbed a number of times."

Sara stared down at the pretty victim, shook her head and said, "Why? Why kill her?"

"That, my dear friend, is for you to find out."

Carla stepped forward and stood beside Sara. "Lorraine, would you say there are similarities between this and the recent rape-kill case we're working on?"

Sara faced her partner. "You're right." She turned to the pathologist and waited for her answer. "She's spot on, isn't she?" Sara prompted when Lorraine didn't answer right away.

"To me, yes, there's no doubt in my mind."

Sara bashed a fist against her thigh. "I fucking knew it. This means that the wrong man has been sent to prison."

"Whoa! Wait just a minute, you can't be sure of that," Carla jumped in.

"Can't I? Zappel was resolute he didn't commit the second murder. If you remember back to the interview, he appeared bloody shocked when I even mentioned the incident."

"So, what are we saying? There were two murderers out there?" Carla said on a heavy sigh.

"Seems that way to me. Jesus, Lorraine, the DNA, can you get that sample dealt with ASAP? I mean, as in get it to the lab within the next thirty minutes for me?"

Lorraine got to work with her equipment. She took the sample, placed it in an evidence bag and sealed it. Then she summoned a member of her team. "Stuart, get this over to the lab, quickly. Instruct them to drop everything and to get the results back to me today, if at all possible."

"On my way now, boss." The man jumped in a van and tore away from the crime scene.

"Thanks, Lorraine. I appreciate it. I'm so cut up about this. I'm guilty of taking my eye off the ball for a second or two, and this is the bloody result. This woman's death was an unnecessary consequence of an ongoing investigation that I should have dealt with properly. I feel sick to the stomach."

Lorraine placed a consoling arm around her shoulder. "Don't you dare go down that route, Sara, you hear me? You're not to blame. The only person who should feel any guilt or responsibility, should be the killer."

"It's not going to help, Lorraine. This is down to me. I should have listened to the suspect."

"I won't have you beating yourself up like this, Sara. Suspects deny their involvement in crimes all the time. It's natural for them. You mustn't blame yourself for this, you hear me?"

"I hear you, but it's not going to alter the devastating feeling running through me. I'm to blame, there's no getting away from that, no matter what type of spin you put on it."

Carla sighed. "You're wrong, Sara. None of this is down to you, to *us* even, I was in the interview room with you, remember? If you're blaming yourself, then you should be apportioning some of that blame on me as well. Neither of us could have predicted this happening."

"But we both had doubts. After the interview with Zappel, we got the team doing extra research. It was there in my mind all along that he was innocent, of the murders anyway."

"Listen to yourself." Carla shook her by the shoulders. "You're wrong. We've done everything we could to get to the truth. I will not stand back and watch you punish yourself like this."

Lorraine applauded. "I'm with Carla on this one. Don't do this, Sara."

Sara held her hands up. "All right, you two. I get the message. Back off or you're going to have me in tears and you know, once I start, I won't be able to stop."

Carla and Lorraine high-fived. "Good," Carla said. "What now?"

"We need to question the woman who found her. Sorry, I should have asked, Lorraine, any ID on the vic?"

"Yep, a bank card with her name on it. No driving licence from what I could see in her bag, maybe that's why she was walking. Casey Nugent, I'm thinking she works at the hospital, I might be guilty of overthinking that notion though." Lorraine winked at Sara.

"Funny, I know you only said that to cheer me up."

"It worked, right?" Lorraine countered.

"It did. Now you girls have stopped ganging up on me, we should get cracking with the investigation, Carla. Unless there's anything else you need to share with us, Lorraine?"

"Nope, all good here. I'll get on with the further examination and then get her shifted back to the mortuary."

"Thanks. Ring me with the results."

"I will, it goes without saying. I'll keep hounding the tech guys for the DNA results, to ease the pressure on you."

"That's brilliant. Thanks for the pep talk, or should I say boot up the arse?"

Lorraine smiled. "Always a pleasure."

Sara and Carla left the scene but kept their protective suits on. "I can't believe it," Sara mumbled.

"Don't go there, Sara. We've been over this. There's no point blaming yourself. All we can do is double our efforts and find the bastard responsible."

"I know how it works," Sara snapped back. She faced Carla, whose head dropped. "Sorry, I didn't mean to have a go." She forced her shoulders back, determined in her quest.

A woman was standing at the window of the house they were after. She waved at them as they climbed the three steps up to the front door. She opened it and greeted them through tearful eyes. "Hello, you must be the police."

"We are. DI Sara Ramsey and DS Carla Jameson. Pleased to meet you, Miss Martin."

"Thanks, it's Mrs, but please, call me Lizzie. Do you want to come in?" she asked, pointing at their suits.

"No, we're fine as we are. What can you tell us regarding the victim?"

"I found her when I came home from my night shift. I wasn't feeling too well, so my line manager sent me home early. I got home around four-fifteen, parked my car in the garage and was walking back. God, I nearly tripped over her, I was distracted, using my phone at the time. I rang nine-nine-nine straight away. I didn't even touch her, well, I could tell she was dead, the way she was lying there with her eyes open."

"It must have been a shock for you. So glad you rang us as soon as you found her. Did you happen to see anyone in the area around that time?"

"No, I can't say I did, sorry. I've gone over what happened several times, more than that even, and well, nothing is coming to mind. I'm so glad the murderer wasn't still around when I got home, that's all I can say." She shuddered at the prospect.

"You were lucky, that's for sure. Is your husband in?"

"No, that toe-rag left me a few months ago. Shacked up with a bitch from the Plough Inn up the road. He's got sex and beer on tap now, I shouldn't wonder, nectar from the gods for a man like him. Bastard has been cheating on me since the day he slipped the wedding ring on my finger."

"Sorry to hear that. Is there anyone else in the house? Someone who might have either heard or seen anything perhaps?"

"No. I live alone. You'll need to try the other neighbours, might be a bit early for some of them though."

Sara glanced at her watch, it was just after six a.m. "Hmm... okay, we'll leave it for now. I'll send a uniformed officer around later to take a statement from you, if that's okay?"

"Can you make it later this afternoon? I was hoping to catch a few hours' sleep before I go to work this evening."

"Of course. How about five o'clock, will that suit you?"

"Perfect. Providing I can sleep after seeing her dead like that."

"I know. You're going to need to block it out. It's not the most pleasant thing in the world to witness. Thanks for your help."

"Too right. Who do you think did it?"

Sara had started walking back down the steps. She turned once she was at the bottom and shrugged. "Without any witnesses, it's hard to say."

"Gosh, I don't envy you your job then. I hope you catch the bastard soon, for all our sakes."

"Thanks. I'm sure we will." Sara and Carla walked back towards the crime scene. "She's right about one thing, it's too early to start canvassing the area. Let's get uniform to do that for us. I'll organise it once we get back to the station, later. I'm in dire need of a coffee, left the house this morning without my usual fix," Sara said.

"Me too. There's an all-night café around the corner, if you're up for it. Mind you, it's a bit rough."

"As long as the coffee is good, I don't care. Let's strip off first." They slipped off their suits and threw them in the crime scene black bag. Sara sought out Lorraine again. "We had a word with Mrs Martin, got the ins and outs of her failed marriage to her cheating husband, but very little else. We're going to head off now."

"I bet that was a joy to hear. Okay, I'll be in touch soon. Remember, no self-recriminations, okay?"

"Yes, yes. I promise. Speak to you later."

Sara followed Carla back to her car. "You'll have to lead the way. I don't have a clue where I'm going."

"If we park at the end of this road, we can set off on foot. It's not too far to walk."

"Sounds good to me."

They jumped in their respective cars and drove up the road, pulled over and joined up again to continue the rest of the journey on foot. Sara's stomach rumbled. "Have you ever eaten at this place?"

"No. But I know plenty who have and who can vouch for its food."

"That's good enough for me. Fancy a fry-up?"

"Yum, a fry-up in a greasy spoon to start our day, why not?" Carla said, an unexpected note of sarcasm edging her tone.

"That told me. The choice is yours. I'm going to need something substantial to see me through the rest of the day."

"I don't know where you put it. You never pile on the weight either."

"That's debatable. I'd go into how I manage to burn off calories every day, but I'll spare your blushes."

Carla laughed. "You're such a bragger at times, without even realising you're doing it."

Sara chuckled. "I knew exactly what I was saying. Let's see what this place has to offer, then."

They walked in and Sara felt out of place immediately. The tables were full of what appeared to be builders, judging by the state of their clothes. Every one of the men watched them take their seats at the table. A petite woman in her early fifties came over to the table before they'd even had a chance to look at the menu propped up between the salt and pepper pots.

"What can I get you, ladies?" She held a notepad and pen, awaiting their response; at the same time, her foot started tapping on the tiled floor.

"Two white coffees with one sugar to start with. What do you recommend?"

"Oh, right, yeah, the full English is what we're the most famous for. You want everything with that?"

"What does it include?" Sara asked, at the same time running a finger around her waistband to see if there was any room for the upcoming onslaught.

"Usual—bacon, sausage, fried eggs, beans, black pudding, fried bread plus toast. Is that all right?"

"Sounds fantastic, everything but black pudding for me. No offence, it's just not something I've enjoyed in the past."

"Whatever. Each to their own. What about you?" The waitress pointed her pen at Carla.

"I'll have the same as she's having. Thanks."

"Good choice, except you're going to regret not having the black pudding. I'll be back in a mo with your coffees."

"Thanks," Sara replied. She watched the woman go back behind the counter and then wagged her finger at Carla. "You should be ashamed of yourself, turning down the black pudding."

Carla raised her eyebrows. "Only following your lead, boss. I'm shuddering at the thought of eating it. I did try it once and thought it was foul. Not going there again anytime soon."

The coffee arrived a few moments later, as promised. There was no faulting the quality of the service. Sara found herself running a paper serviette around the side of her cup.

"What are you doing? Stop it. She's coming this way," Carla warned in a hushed voice.

The waitress put their breakfasts down on sparkling clean plates. "Any sauces? Your toast is just coming."

"Ketchup for me, thanks," Sara replied.

"Yeah, me too."

The waitress left and returned with four rounds of toast and a bottle of Heinz ketchup which she placed in the centre of the table. "There you go. Enjoy." She took two paces then flung over her shoulder, "Oh, and by the way, we rinse and double rinse all the cups, always have done, so there's really no need for you to wipe them again, lovey." The waitress marched off.

Laughter reverberated all around them and Sara's cheeks flushed. "Crap, was I that obvious? It's just a habit of mine, I do it everywhere, you know, since the bloody pandemic."

Carla sniggered and squirted her breakfast with ketchup. "Well, I did try and warn you. Thanks for embarrassing us like that."

"Shit, sorry. I'm going to apologise to her after we've eaten."

"I wouldn't bother. Tuck in before it gets cold." Carla took a mouthful of sausage and moaned. "Oh my God, I haven't tasted anything this good in bloody ages."

Sara tried hers and let out a satisfied moan of her own. "You're not wrong. Crap, we can't afford this to be a regular haunt of ours, we'd soon end up looking like some of these guys."

Carla almost choked on the coffee she'd just taken a sip of. "Haven't you dished out enough insults for today? You keep saying things like that and we'll get thrown out."

"I didn't mean anything by it. It was only an observation. It is delicious, good choice coming here. Why haven't you mentioned this place before?"

"It never occurred to me. We were up the road and it just came to mind. Shh... I want to eat it while it's still hot."

They both fell silent and finished off what was sitting on their plates, after which, Sara picked up a slice of toast slathered in butter and nibbled on it.

"You can't be serious?" Carla said, puffing out her cheeks and leaning back in her chair.

"What? I hate wasting food. It's good, proper bread. I wonder if they bake it on the premises."

"I suppose you could ask her that when you go up and apologise."

Sara pulled a face at her partner and continued to eat the chunk of toast. She pushed the rest away and downed the remainder of her coffee. "Best breakfast or meal out I've had in ages."

"Glad to hear you say that," the waitress said, appearing beside her to clear their plates.

"I have an apology to make. I didn't mean to cause offence, I do that everywhere I go, you know, since the pandemic."

"No need to apologise. Glad you enjoyed it. Fancy a Danish pastry for afters?"

"God, no. We're stuffed. Can I get the bill?"

"Come to the counter to pay, lovey."

Sara followed her over and paid a paltry three pounds fifty each for their breakfast. "That can't be right. Here, take a tenner. Keep the change."

The woman smiled. "Why thank you kindly. Maybe we'll see you again one day."

"That's guaranteed. Again, I'm sorry if I upset you."

The woman's smile broadened. "You didn't. See you soon."

They left and walked back to the cars. "Why don't we use one car for now—mine, and pick yours up after we've been to the hospital?"

"Makes sense, it's always a nightmare parking around there."

Sara zapped her doors open and they both got in. During the short journey her phone rang. "Hello, DI Ramsey."

"Sorry to trouble you, ma'am, it's Jeff. I've just come on duty and wanted to bring you up to date on a few things which occurred during the night, one of which, I think, might be relevant to your investigation."

"I'm all ears, Jeff."

"I know you're dealing with a rape-murder at present and all that entails, give me a shout if I can be of any assistance in that matter, by the way."

"You can. You can get a few of your men doing a house-to-house down there, it was too early for us to start banging on doors. See if anyone either saw or heard anything out of the ordinary. What else has come in?"

"I'll get on it after I've spoken to you. I've got a knife crime in which the suspect stole the victim's car, in front of his wife. She's with him at the hospital now. It's touch and go by the look of things. The victim was stabbed in the back, I doubt if he saw his attacker, but his wife did. She rang the station during the night, once her husband was settled, and said she's eager to help identify the culprit."

"Wow, that's excellent news. Okay, well, as it happens, we're just on our way to the hospital now. The victim was a nurse, we've got her name, but that's about all right now. We'll go and see the woman and her husband while we're there. What are their names?"

"He's Mike Stand, wife is Ellen. She's beside herself, as you can imagine."

"Okay, leave it with us."

"Thanks, ma'am. I'll get my guys out there to begin knocking on the doors within a couple of hours."

"Let me know as soon as you hear anything. We need to up our game in catching this bastard, he's clearly upped his by attacking one and killing another on the same night."

"I'll call you as soon as I hear anything."

"Thanks, Jeff." Sara ended the call.

"So, his intention was to steal the man's vehicle. He's got away with that so far. Did he rape and kill the nurse before that attack or after?" Carla asked.

Sara briefly turned her way as she drove. "Interesting, right? Until Lorraine gives us an estimated time of death for the victim, all we're going to have to go on is what the wife tells us when we get there."

"Either way, I sense we're in for a busy day."

"You're not wrong." Sara indicated and pulled into the hospital car park. The barrier rose allowing her access. They dashed through the main entrance. Sara flashed her warrant card at the brunette sitting at the reception desk. "We're here about two things. One is to question a husband and wife about a stabbing incident which occurred last night. The victim's name is Mike Stand."

"Ah yes, I recognise the name, I've just processed the paperwork for his admittance. Give me a second to source where they've taken him."

Sara smiled and nodded.

"Here it is. He's due to go down to surgery soon. Therefore, he'll still be waiting in the A&E department. Which is along the corridor on the right, at the end."

"Super, thanks for that. Also, we're looking for information about a nurse who possibly works here, Casey Nugent, do you know her?"

"Gosh, let me think. We have so many nurses on the staff, it's hard to keep up with the new arrivals. Let me ask around for you."

"That would be brilliant. Thank you." They took a step back, allowing the receptionist to place the calls she needed without them bearing down on her.

The receptionist ended her first call and smiled, then immediately placed another. This time she nodded and beckoned Sara and Carla towards her. "I've managed to track her down, she's a student in the maternity unit, on the second floor."

"Thanks, we'll drop in after we've been to A&E."

"You're welcome."

They raced up the corridor. Once they reached A&E, they surveyed the surrounding area. "Why don't we split up? If he's awaiting surgery, my guess is he'll be in one of the cubicles. I'll start this end and we'll meet in the middle."

Carla set off to the other end, and they worked their way down the long row of cubicles until Carla coughed to gain her attention. Sara raced to the other end of the hallway. Pulling back the curtain to the only cubicle occupied by a couple, they found Ellen Stand, sitting by her husband's bedside. She had tear-stained cheeks and was shaking her head. She seemed confused and petrified at the same time.

Sara produced her ID. "Mrs Stand, we're DI Sara Ramsey and DS Carla Jameson. I'm sorry to hear what happened to your husband, how's he doing?"

"Not good. He was stabbed in the back several times. They're telling me he might not make it through the surgery. I won't be able to live without him, he's my world."

"I'm sorry. Try to think positively about the outcome, doctors have been known to get it wrong occasionally. Are you up to answering a few questions?"

"Why not? It's not as if I've got anything better to do, is it?"

Sara stood on the opposite side of the bed and glanced briefly at the woman's injured husband. "Can you tell us what happened?"

Sara saw Carla flip out her notebook and pen out of her peripheral vision.

Mrs Stand inhaled a large breath and let it out. Her chest rose and fell in the process. She didn't take her eyes off her husband who was lying unconscious in the bed. "Mike had just come home. He parked the car and got out. He seemed distracted, I think with his phone. I was looking out of the window, waiting for him. Suddenly, this man appeared out of nowhere and stabbed my husband in the back..." She paused, swallowed as if to compose herself and continued, "I shot out of the house, shouted at him and ran towards my husband. I didn't care that the man might attack me, all I wanted to do was make sure Mike was okay. The man grabbed the car keys from Mike and jumped in the car. I couldn't give a damn; a car is replaceable, my husband on the other hand is not. We've been together almost twenty years. He can't die, I won't allow him to."

Sara patted her on the arm. "Stay strong and remain positive. Did you get a look at the man?"

"Yes, I told your guys when I rang up that I could ID him if you wanted me to. You know, with one of those sketch artists. I want this man caught, he needs to be punished for incapacitating my husband like this."

"He does. Maybe you can give us a brief description now to get the ball rolling, it might take a little time to organise a sketch artist, depending how busy they are. Would that be possible?"

"Of course. He was youngish, around twenty-five to thirty. He had dark brown hair, it may have even been black. A larger than average nose with tiny eyes. I'm sorry, I was too far away and the lighting wasn't that brilliant to make out what colour his eyes were."

"That's okay. You're doing well. What about his height and build?"

"Well, Mike is six-foot-one, the attacker was around that mark, maybe slightly smaller, but only by a few inches, does that make sense?"

"Yes, so around five-ten or five-eleven perhaps?"

"Yes, now why didn't I say that?"

"It's okay. You're forgiven under the circumstances. What type of build would you say he was?"

"Slim. Not an ounce of fat on him, borderline skinny, I suppose you'd call him."

"That's excellent. Could you make out what type of clothes he had on?"

"Dark as in a dark sweatshirt, might even have been a hoodie. If it was, then it begs the question why he didn't use it."

"It does. Maybe attacking your husband was a spur of the moment type of thing, he would have been more prepared had the attack been premeditated."

"I suppose. I think he had black trousers on, the fleecy type, what are they called? Ah yes, jogging pants. Mike had some years ago when he used to work out at the gym. In the days, he used to feel the need to impress me." She ran a hand over her husband's protruding pot belly. "Those days are long gone. Still, I love him for who he is, not for an athletic physique which would take hours down at the gym to maintain."

"Did the perpetrator speak at all when you shouted at him? Maybe he had a dialect which you picked up on?"

"No. He glared at me, got in the car and drove off. I was more concerned about Mike and didn't try to run after him or tackle him, if that's what you're asking."

"I see. Well, I think we have enough to be going on with. I know the desk sergeant has issued an alert for your husband's car. As soon as we have any news regarding the vehicle, and the availability of the sketch artist, we'll be in touch. Wishing your husband well. He'll be in our thoughts."

"Thank you. Please, please get this man. He shouldn't be allowed to roam the streets, picking on innocent victims and robbing them of their possessions. If he's stolen Mike from me, I'll..." Her voice drifted off and tears dripped down her cheeks. "I'm sorry. I keep telling myself not to break down in case he can hear me. I want to remain positive, if that will help see him through this."

"You're doing the right thing. We'll leave you to it and be in touch as things progress. Good luck."

Ellen smiled and then glanced lovingly at her husband again.

Sara and Carla left the cubicle and didn't speak until they were a few feet away. "I need to call the information in." She peered at her watch. "The team should be getting into work about now. I'll give them a call and apprise them of the situation."

She rang the incident room. Christine picked up. "Hi, boss. Where are you?"

"At the hospital. We've been at it since around five. I need you to take down this information and get it circulated ASAP, Christine. I sense we're closing in on this bastard." She read out the description of the perpetrator and gave a brief rundown on the events they'd been dealing with since the crack of dawn.

"You should have rung me, boss. I would have come in and manned the incident room for you."

"As kind as that offer is, Christine, there really was no need. We're on another mission now, to track down the next of kin for the nurse. After that, we'll go break the news and then come back to base."

"Good luck. We'll see you soon."

Sara ended the call. "Let's get this over with. Bloody hell, I'm knackered already and it's only nine."

"Yep, plodding on. We're going to be dead on our feet by lunchtime."

"I fear you could be right. What we need is a double dose of caffeine, but that's not likely to happen for a while."

They sought out the lift and took it up to the second floor. The maternity ward was at the end of the corridor, not a place Sara had ever visited since moving to the area and she had no personal plans to visit it in the future either. "Here we go. Let's get gelled up."

Entering the ward, they made a beeline for the nurses' station halfway up. Sara showed her warrant card. "Hi, I've been told that a Casey Nugent works on this ward."

"That's right. She's not here today. She's due in later though. Can I help you with anything?"

"We're hoping you'll give us her address, or that of her next of kin, if you have it on record?"

The Ward Sister frowned. "Oh my, why on earth would you need her next of kin? Has something happened to her? Please, she's part of our team, if there's something wrong, I'd like to know."

Sara didn't feel inclined to hold back. It was important the emergency services were open and honest with each other. She lowered her voice to just above a whisper. "Sadly, Casey lost her life last night in a brutal attack."

The Sister clamped a hand over her mouth and dropped into the chair behind her. Carla raced around the desk to make sure she was okay. The woman waved her away.

"I'm fine. I think. How could someone do this to her? She was such a wonderful young woman with such a bright future ahead of her. A star pupil in many people's eyes. This is so unfair."

Another nurse appeared and asked, "Is something wrong?"

"It's Casey, she's dead."

The other nurse gasped and slapped a hand to her cheek. "No, no, no! How can she be dead?"

"Please, I must ask you to keep this information between yourselves for the time being. At least, until the family have been informed. As I said, that's why we're here, to try and get her next of kin details. Can you help?"

The Ward Sister nodded and left her chair. She gripped hold of the desk and Carla helped to steady her. "Take it slowly, you've had a shock."

"Thanks, I'll be fine. I'm eager to get the information for you. This is too terrible for words. I'm appalled this should happen to one of our own." She opened a filing cabinet at the back of the area and pulled out a file. "I insisted on us having our own copies of family details, just in case anything happened while any of our nurses were on shift. Not every ward has them, you understand."

"I'm glad you do," Sara replied.

The woman returned to the reception desk and placed the folder on the counter. Carla jotted down the details of Casey's parents' address and returned to the other side of the counter to stand next to Sara.

"Thank you. We'll shoot over there now and bring them up to date."

"Wait. You have to tell us how she died."

Sara noticed the photos on the wall of the nurses who worked on this particular ward, each of them smiling, looking proud to be wearing their uniform. "She was stabbed and left for dead. We're dealing with a few similar cases in the area. Looks like she was in the wrong place at the wrong time, I'm sorry."

"As long as she wasn't raped. Can't bear the thought of her going through that ordeal before she took her final breath. Not that being stabbed isn't bad enough. Oh bugger, I'm getting myself all mixed up. I didn't mean it to come out that way."

"No need to apologise." Sara didn't have the heart to confide in the woman about the rape. Instead, she thanked her and left the ward.

They were in the lift when some form of alarm went off. "Shit, is that a fire alarm? Crap, and we're stuck in a lift. Not frigging ideal."

Carla gripped her forearm. "Calm down. We're almost there now."

The doors opened, and they sprinted out towards the main entrance. People were in panic mode. Nervously glancing around them and dithering about which way to run for the best.

Sara stopped at the reception desk. "What's going on? Is there a fire?"

"No. There's been an incident in A&E. Someone got in there with a knife."

Sara faced Carla and they both bolted at the same time. They reached A&E within a few moments. Nurses and porters were darting around, trying to allay everyone's fears. Sara grabbed a porter as he passed and showed her ID. "What's the problem?"

"A man strolled in off the street, wielding a knife. He ran through the area, pulling at the curtains, obviously trying to find someone."

"Shit! Did he find who he was looking for?"

"No. I don't think so. As soon as the alarm went off, he panicked and ran for the exit."

"Did anyone go after him?"

"Are you kidding me? No, why would we put our lives in danger like that?" the porter replied, his voice high-pitched with anxiety.

"Okay. I only asked. I'm trying to do my job quickly and efficiently. I haven't got time to argue with you when a madman is on the loose." She hesitated for a moment to ponder whether she should check on the patient, but her need to catch the criminal won her inner battle.

"Sorry. Please, you need to get after him and stop arguing with me."

Sara and Carla started running. "How long ago?" Sara called over her shoulder.

"As soon as the alarm kicked off."

"Okay. Thanks."

They sped back through the corridor and out of the main entrance. En route, Sara called the station for backup. Once they were outside, she and Carla took off in different directions. "He could still be lying in wait out here. Ring me if you see him and for God's sake, stay vigilant and be careful."

"Ditto, if you lay eyes on him first." Carla shot off and weaved through the two cars closest to her.

Sara scoured the area around the car park. She asked the attendant if he'd seen anything whilst sitting in his little hut. He said he saw a man run out of the hospital and get in a car, but it was too far for him to work out what make the car was.

"Which direction did he go?"

The man grinned. "The same direction all the traffic goes when it leaves here, there's only one way out or hadn't you noticed that? Where's the fire anyway?" He lifted his mug and took a sip.

Sara mumbled a reluctant thanks for the little help he'd offered and made her way over to the car.

"'Ere, don't you go forgetting to pay before you get in your vehicle."

Seething, she stormed across the car park to the machine by his hut. "You're kidding me? Three pounds fifty for a five-minute stay. Now I know someone is taking the piss! Can't you let me off? I'm trying to apprehend a dangerous criminal."

"More than my job's worth. Dig deep in that purse of yours, it's well known how tight you coppers are."

"For fuck's sake!" Sara muttered. She found the correct coins, thrust them into the damn machine and ran back to the car, not bothering to speak to the obtuse man again.

The barrier raised after a lengthy delay, no doubt that had been on purpose too, and she set off, glancing around to find Carla. She wasn't around. Sara rang her mobile on the hands-free. "Pick up the damn phone, will you?"

Nothing. Carla didn't answer.

Sara's breakfast reappeared and lodged itself in the back of her throat.

"Jesus! Please, don't tell me he's taken her."

10

*S*ara returned to the station. She flew through the reception area and up to the incident room to find DCI Price waiting for her. "Jesus, I've just heard. Have you had any contact with Carla at all?"

Tearful, Sara ran a hand through her hair and perched on the nearest desk. "No. One minute she was there and the next she was gone. Why the fuck did we split up? This is all my fault."

The chief gripped her by the upper arms and shook her slightly. "Stop it! You hear me? You're not to blame. Tell me what happened. Wait, someone get DI Ramsey a cup of coffee, make it snappy."

Craig burst out of his seat and returned to place the cup in front of Sara.

"Thanks, Craig." She took a sip of the boiling hot liquid, scalded her tongue and set the cup down again. "We were at the hospital, getting the next of kin details for the latest victim… shit, I still have to deal with that."

"It's fine. I'll get someone else on it. Carry on, what happened next?" the chief asked.

Tears pricked as Sara recalled the events. She covered her eyes with her hands, determined not to let the rest of the team see her break down.

The chief recognised the personal torment she was putting herself through. "Would you rather do this in private, in your office?"

"No. I'll be fine. Everyone needs to hear this to know what we're up against. We need to organise the troops, get uniform out there searching for her and this... madman. Oh God, I can't believe I took my eye off the ball and allowed this to happen. Poor Carla! What if...?"

"Don't you dare go there, stop blaming yourself for this, Inspector, you hear me? You're obviously up against a determined criminal who doesn't give a shit about upsetting people in authority."

"He's an unknown quantity. I'm bloody livid this has happened. Livid and tormented with fear. He's killed three people, possibly, and put another one in hospital. That's why he was there. The staff at A&E raised the alarm because a man entered brandishing a knife, searching for someone. I believe he went there with the intention of killing the victim, not wanting to leave any loose ends." Her voice drifted off as the tears started to roll down her cheeks. "Christ, Carla, where are you? Please, be safe."

"Okay, I've seen and heard enough, Sara, I have to pull you off the case."

Sara glanced up at the chief. Her mouth dropped open to speak but nothing came out.

The chief went on, "I'm calling in another Inspector to take over. For your benefit as well as Carla's. It's what's best in the circumstances, believe me. You won't be thinking straight, under the pressure. This way, we're giving Carla the best chance we can."

Sara's gaze circulated the room. The rest of the team were all nodding, obviously agreeing with the chief. "If I don't have a say in this, then so be it. But, by Christ, if whoever you bring in screws up, I'll have his testicles removed by a lion at the nearest zoo. That's not a threat, that's a damn promise."

The chief laughed. "What if your replacement turns out to be female?"

"Then I'll do the same with her tits. I still want to register my discontent about this situation, though. If you gave me a few minutes' grace, I'd be up and running on full steam again. If someone else is responsible for putting Carla's life in further danger, I will take retribution."

"Talking like that isn't helpful, Sara. Pack it in, that's an order. Give me an hour to sort something out. I have someone in mind, but he may need to travel."

"Oh crap! Really? We need someone here now, not in a few hours, boss. Now!"

"I understand that. Wind your neck in and let me get on with it. Until then, are you up to going over things with the team? To guide them what to do next?"

"*H*onest answer, yes, in a few minutes. Which is why we won't need anyone else. Carla is not only my partner, she's a dear friend as well. You really think I'd purposefully make the wrong move and endanger her life further? That's bullshit. If you think that low of me, then maybe I shouldn't be in the job in the first place, boss."

"Jesus! Not now, Sara. Please don't insinuate that. Let me get on the phone and organise things. I'll get back to you soon." The chief rushed out of the room.

Christine was the first to speak when the door shut behind the chief. "Are you all right, boss?"

"To be honest, I feel absolutely numb. Maybe the boss has made the right call, bringing in an outsider to deal with this. I know it's not going to be easy working under someone else, but let's give it our best shot, agreed?"

The team either shouted back 'agreed' or 'okay'. "Good. I'm going to go through what happened, and hope I don't leave anything out. After that, I'm going to need a volunteer to go to the nurse's next of kin for me. Preferably female."

Marissa raised her hand. "I'll go."

"Good, thanks, love. Craig, why don't you go with her? Please, let Marissa do the talking. We need to be sensitive about this, I'm not saying you're not. And for goodness' sake, please be evasive with the circumstances of her death. Do not mention the rape at this point. That's not how we do things, got that?"

Marissa and Craig both nodded.

"Shit! Carla has the information for the next of kin. Marissa, ring the maternity ward at the hospital and ask for the information again. Come up with some excuse as to why you're contacting them a second time within a few hours. God, this is such a mess. Please, please Carla, be okay."

Marissa reached for the phone to put in the request and hung up a few minutes later. "I've got it, boss."

"Good. You two set off. Keep your eyes peeled while you're out there."

Chairs scraped and they both put their jackets on. "We will," Craig announced.

Once the two young detectives had left, Sara took a sip of her now cool coffee and paced the room. "Where do we start? Why did this happen? We were chasing him, not the other way round. How the fuck did he get hold of her in the first place? Why her and not me? Why, why, why?"

"There's no point in you blaming yourself, boss, that's self-destructive and isn't going to get us anywhere," Christine was quick to jump in.

"I know. But I'm at a loss what to think or how to put things right. We have no idea who we're dealing with here. What if he kidnaps her and takes her out of the city? Or, what if he's taken her and she gives him some lip and he…"

"Please, don't say it, boss. Don't even think it. Carla is made of strong stuff. She knows when to keep her mouth shut. She'll be fine, we have to believe that," Jill piped up.

"I hope you're both right. Damn, we can deal with this between us. I'm going to see the chief, tell her we're up to the task. I'll be right back."

Sara pushed open the door and marched up the corridor. The DCI's secretary, Mary, greeted her with a warm smile.

"Hello, Inspector Ramsey. How are you?"

"I've had better days, Mary. Can I go through?"

"Let me just check with her. She's been tied up on the phone since she returned." Mary shot out of her seat, knocked on the door, then popped her head into the room. "DI Ramsey here to see you, ma'am, if you have a minute."

"Two minutes, then send her in. I'm almost done here."

Mary retreated from the room and retook her seat. "She won't be too long. Take the weight off."

She gestured for Sara to sit, but she was far too anxious and paced the room until the chief's door opened. "In here, Inspector."

Sara raced through the open doorway and took a seat in front of the chief. "Have you made any arrangements yet?"

"Yes, just this second finalised something. Why?"

"Call whoever it is off. I can deal with it. My team and I have discussed it and we're up to the job in hand," Sara said, lying through her back teeth.

"While I think that's admirable for you to say, my decision is final. There's no going back now. Des Williams is coming over from Worcester. He'll be here within the hour and is itching to sink his teeth in."

"Jesus! Were those his words or yours?"

"Mine, why? Oh, stop being so defensive all the time, Sara."

"How do you expect me to react? Carla will be relying on me to get her out of this fix, *alive,* and that responsibility has been stripped from me and passed on to someone else neither of us knows."

"But I do. By the sounds of it, you're doubting my capabilities as a DCI."

"Now you're twisting my words, I didn't say that, boss. I'm sorry if it came across that way. All I'm guilty of doing is trying to get my partner back before something bad or even worse happens to her." Sara's voice rose as she spoke.

The DCI pointed a finger at her. "I'm warning you to calm down. Take a few steady breaths."

She did as she was ordered and held her head in shame. "I'm sorry. Surely, you can put yourself in my shoes for a moment or two."

"Absolutely. Carla is not only your partner, she's also a member of my team, you seem to have forgotten that, Sara. I need you to take a step back and assess the situation with clear and concise thoughts if we're ever going to get her back from this criminal. That's why it's better for you not to be involved in the case. As well as it being procedure in these instances, anyway."

Sara's shoulders slumped in defeat. "I'm sorry. You're right, of course. It's just difficult sitting on one's hands when you know a frigging madman could be doing all sorts to your partner and friend."

"I appreciate that, I promise I do. You need to rid yourself of such thoughts; otherwise, you're going to make yourself ill and then you'll be no use to anyone, either during the investigation or afterwards. Now, what do we know about this man?"

"The man who's got her?"

"Yes. Apart from the murders he's committed. Wait, how many cases are you dealing with concerning this culprit?"

"That's just it, I don't know for sure. We've arrested Zappel for the first crime at least. He kept telling me he wasn't involved with the second murder, but the evidence was there for us all to see. Now, I'm not so sure."

"What evidence are we talking about here?"

"Zappel was seen taking money from the first victim's bank account by the ATM cameras and his car was spotted close to the scene of the second crime. Therefore, we put two and two together and banged him up for it."

"Wait. You actually saw the man's face?"

"No." Sara sighed. "When we went to pick him up, he pointed out his hat and coat. In the images, the person was wearing the same outfit. I asked Zappel if anyone had access to his car, and he assured me that no one did. It was a natural decision to take the route I did, wasn't it?"

"I suppose so. It's a bit light to say the least, Sara, we'll find out if the evidence is good enough once we get to court."

Sara shuffled her feet, suddenly feeling uncomfortable under the chief's scrutinising glare. "If I've screwed up, I'm sorry. If all this is down to me, then I'll hand in my notice right away."

"Now you're being bloody ridiculous. What other evidence do you have? The second victim was raped, wasn't she? Any semen found at the scene or on her body?"

"I'm still waiting for the PM results."

"What about the victim last night? Shall we call her victim number three for now?"

"Yes, the pathologist believes the culprit cocked up and left semen in the woman's body."

"I see. Well, that's one piece of good news, isn't it?"

"I suppose," Sara reluctantly agreed.

The chief tilted her head. "If he's had a record for previous crimes of this nature, then his DNA will be on our database, we're all aware of how this works, aren't we?"

"True enough. Do I have your permission to keep chasing the pathology department with regard to our initial investigations?"

"Of course. Des Williams is coming on board to oversee Carla's disappearance only, although I suspect the two will overlap at some point."

"That's what I'm worried about."

"Don't be. If he becomes too much, point him in my direction and I'll sort him out. At the end of the day, you need to treat him as a friend and not the enemy, got that?"

"I understand. I hate not being in control, though. Surely you can understand that?"

"Of course I do. You wouldn't be human if you didn't feel that way. Now, shoo. Get out of here."

Sara smiled and jumped out of her chair. "Thanks for listening."

She returned to the incident room, feeling deflated and unsure how to proceed with the investigation which had blighted their lives all week. *You need to get a grip, girl. Get this killer off the streets. Shit!*

This killer has Carla. How the fuck are we going to get her back when we don't know who the bastard is?

A nugget of an idea sparked, and she stormed into her office to ring the prison. She was put through to Governor Prentice at Usk prison, where Zappel was being held temporarily on remand.

"Hello, Governor. I'm DI Sara Ramsey of the West Mercia Police, based in Hereford."

"Hello, Inspector, what can I do for you?"

Sara warmed to the woman from the amiable timbre in her voice. "Hi, one of the criminals I arrested this week is on remand with you, I wondered if it would be possible to pay him a visit today."

"Today? Any specific reason for this great urgency?"

"There is. Since his arrest, similar crimes have been committed on my patch and I need to know if he has an inkling why."

"I see. Did you not question him fully while he was in your custody, Inspector?"

Sara sighed. "The questions were asked, but periodically he went down the 'no comment' route, which was frustrating as hell, as you can imagine. Since then, we've had several more crimes occur, similar to those we thought he was responsible for. Which has got me thinking that he may either have had an accomplice or we have a copycat killer on our hands. The urgency to find this person has escalated in the past hour or so, since the culprit kidnapped my partner."

"I see. Cruel and devastating circumstances to deal with. Of course, I can authorise a visit for you. When do you need it?"

"As soon as humanly possible, if that's all right?"

"I'll get on it. Come over when you like, I'll make the guard on the gate aware of your impending visit. Give me a ring if you need anything else from me."

"Thank you. You're too kind. I'll get my arse into gear and be with you within half an hour or so."

"Drive safely."

Sara ended the call. Relieved she wasn't dealing with an overbearing, officious nutjob as a governor, similar to ones she'd come across at her previous post. She darted through the incident room and said,

"Carry on delving into the background details we need for Zapped. I've made arrangements to question him again in prison. An inspector is on his way from Worcester, he's going to be taking over the case regarding Carla's disappearance, which is why I need to run now, before he gets here. Fortunately, the governor took pity on me and issued an invitation to join her and her team. Wish me luck."

"Wait," Christine shouted before Sara could reach the door.

She turned back and asked, "For what? I'm wasting time, Christine."

"Boss, you haven't told us why you're going. What are we supposed to tell the chief when she drops in to introduce us to the new inspector?"

"Shit! That's a fair point. I'm following up on a notion I have, what if it's the son we're looking for? I won't know until I speak to Jo. Tell the chief I'm out there combing the streets, retracing my steps from this morning around the area where Carla went missing." She inhaled a large breath then continued, "Actually, just as an aside, Will, can you take a trip out to the last crime scene, see if Carla's car is located at the end of the road? She parked there and came in my car to the hospital. I'm thinking her abductor might have forced the information out of her and switched cars. He's already stolen one car and put the owner of that vehicle in hospital, that's why he was there, at the hospital, to finish him off. The staff in A&E raised the alarm and scared him off. In his panic, he took Carla because we bloody split up in the grounds of the hospital. Shit, sorry, my head's chockful of different scenarios and I should have relayed that information to you sooner. I'm having a shit day, and it's about to go from bad to worse once someone comes marching in here, shouting the odds and taking over."

Will left his seat and tucked his chair under the desk. "I'll get out there right now, boss."

"Good. I should be back within a few hours. Keep your chins up and don't let me down, guys. Carla is out there, her life in mortal danger. I can't sit around here doing sweet fuck all, it's not in me to do that."

"Good luck," Christine shouted as she left the room.

. . .

*T*hirty-five minutes later, after going around the block a few times in search of a blasted parking space, Sara finally found one in the centre of the tiny town of Usk. She raced back to the prison and produced her ID. The guard signed her in and led her down the long winding corridor to the interview room.

"Zappel will be brought in shortly. He'll remain handcuffed throughout, there will also be an officer present during the interview. I hope you're okay with that?"

"I am. Thanks very much. Would I be pushing my luck asking you for a coffee?"

The guard smiled. "I'll get that sorted for you. My advice would be to keep your hand on it throughout, just in case the prisoner tries to use it as a weapon. Stranger things have happened around here, I can assure you."

"Eek... I never even thought about that. I'll be extra vigilant in that case."

Once he left the room, she settled into the chair and scrolled through her phone which had pinged during the drive—she had received a new message. It was from Will. She opened it and saw a picture of Carla's car still parked in the space where they'd left it earlier that morning. That was a relief she hadn't seen coming. The notion had occurred to her that the kidnapper might have used the vehicle to keep them on their toes, possibly switching it for another one when the opportunity arose, trying to keep one step ahead of them. Maybe he'd slipped up there.

Sara sent a message back to Will, thanking him for his effort and that she'd be in touch as soon as she left the prison.

A thumbs-up emoji was sent as his response.

Soon after, the door opened and a tired and browbeaten Zappel walked into the room. The officer guided him to his seat and forced him to sit with a well-placed hand on his shoulder to enforce the move.

"Hello again, Jo. I hope they're treating you well here."

He peered over his shoulder at the officer who was now standing at the rear of the room a few feet behind him. "I can't grumble. I wasn't expecting to see you again. What do you want from me?"

"It was a surprise to me too. Okay, I'm not going to delay this any longer than necessary, I need your help."

He laughed and tipped his head back. When he'd calmed down, he placed his clenched, cuffed hands on the table and looked her in the eye. "With what?"

Sara kept a warm smile in place and told him, "I believe I made a mistake arresting you for both crimes. I'm willing to admit to my faults and have a word with the CPS to get you a lesser sentence."

"Yeah, you don't say. I told you all along I wasn't guilty, but would you listen? Would you fuck—?"

"Oi, Zappel, that's your first warning. No swearing. Two more and you get taken back to your cell, you got that?"

"Yes, sir. Fuck, fuck. That's my three. You can take me back now."

The officer left his position and came towards them. Sara raised a hand. "No, please. This is really important. Won't you waive his behaviour for now? I'm fine with the swearing."

"Well, I'm not. Once more and I take him back. We have rules in place which I'm keen to adhere to and, more importantly, I'm here to ensure he observes them, as well."

"I understand. Jo, I'm pleading with you; if you want a lesser sentence, you'd be wise to listen to what I have to say."

"Go on, then. You've got five minutes and then he can take me back to my cell, whether you're finished or not."

"I hear you. Right, no wasting time from me. I need you to be honest with me. At the first crime scene, you told me you were there, but you didn't kill the victim, is that right?"

"Yep. Next!"

"Then who did?"

His gaze left hers and circled the room.

"Jo, come on. What have you got to lose by telling me?"

He laughed. "Nice try. Next."

For fuck's sake moron. I can tell you're trying to keep something from me. I'm not going to let you win, not with Carla's life in danger.

She pulled her ace card out and laid it on the table. "We know who your associate was at the first crime. I believe he got a taste for killing and has since gone on a spree."

His gaze narrowed. "If that's the case, then why are you here?"

"Because we believe he's taken a very dangerous direction and I'd hate to see Adam get killed by a special armed forces team."

His eyes widened. "You leave my son out of this. He wasn't involved in any of the crimes."

"Really? You truly expect me to believe that? It wouldn't be a case of you being prepared to take the fall for your son, would it?"

He fidgeted in his seat. Sara knew she was on to something. He refused to answer, so she pressed on. "Has he reached out to you since you came in here?"

Again, the prisoner refused to answer.

"Come on, Jo. If you love your son, you'd want to make sure he didn't get harmed when we find him, wouldn't you? Because considering the unbelievably crass choices he's made, as soon as the armed coppers get him in their sight, his life will be over with one squeeze of the trigger. Do you really want that to happen, after you taking the fall for him?"

"What are you going on about? You're talking absolute shite. My son has nothing to do with this. He doesn't even live in the area."

"His address is in the Morecambe Bay area, is it not? See, just so you know I'm not trying to pull a fast one. I know all there is to know about your son."

"Funny that! Why are you here then?"

"Because I want there to be a peaceful end to this. There have been too many deaths this week. Are you aware that he raped and killed another victim last night?"

"No. He wouldn't."

"I'm not lying, I assure you. Come on, Jo. Tell me where he is."

He closed his eyes and his head dropped as if Sara had finally defeated him. "At home. If he's not there, then your guess is as good as mine."

"So he was staying at the house with you?"

"Yes, I've only got a small place. I told him I didn't have a spare room, but he said he'd be comfortable on the couch. So that's where he slept. I can't believe he's killed another one." His shoulders slouched in defeat and he muttered, "He killed that old woman. It was my idea to rob her. He got pissed off when she said there was no money in the house. He went in search of it, found it and killed her for lying to him. We fell out over that. I told him to pack his bags. The next thing I knew, you were knocking on my door and accusing me of all sorts, things I had no knowledge of." He shook his head and wrung his hands. His voice was strained when he spoke again. "I couldn't dob him in, I've only just got him back after years apart. His mother left me and moved out of the area."

"Did he have a violent streak before he moved in with you?"

"No. I don't think so. After he killed that old woman, we went back to my place and he sat there rubbing his hands together, the cash he'd found at her house spread all over the floor. Then he told me this would be the first of many, that we'd be rich in no time at all."

"That's terrible. So he was the one who took the money out of the ATM, who used the old lady's card?"

"Yes, he must have borrowed my coat and hat without my knowledge. As soon as you showed me the image, I knew it was him."

"Why didn't you say anything? Why take the fall for someone like that who, let's face it, you barely know?"

"He's my blood. He has my genes, and that of his fucker of a mother, of course."

The officer took a step forward again, but Sara looked up and shook her head. "Please, don't, I need to question him further."

"Once more, and I'm pulling the plug on this interview. I have my limit and it was reached, a long time ago."

"I understand that. Jo, please, I'm here to try and help save your son, swear again and there will be no going back. The chance will be lost. Do you really want to fail your son in that way?"

"No." He glanced over his shoulder. "I'll behave. It slips out, years of practice, sorry, mate."

"I'm not your mate, got that?"

"Loud and clear." Jo faced Sara again and rolled his eyes.

Despite the anxiety coursing through her veins, Sara had to suppress a laugh caught in her throat. "Is there somewhere else he's likely to go?"

Jo shook his head and wrung his hands tighter until his knuckles turned white. "I can't think of anywhere. Please, you have to believe me. I swear I'd tell you, now I know he's in imminent danger."

"I suppose he has money to burn, he could be anywhere, right? Does he have any other relatives in the area?"

"No, no one."

"What about friends, either old or new?"

He thought the question over for a little while and then answered, "Nope, no one. It was just him and me, until he killed that woman. Bloody hell, why did he do it? She was such a sweetheart, too. I've laid awake in my cell since I got here, wishing I could turn back the clock. I want him found as much as you do before he really gets a taste for going after old people. The thing I can't forgive is the fact he's started raping girls and then killing them. Where the... heck did he get that from?"

"I don't know. I'm going to find out if he's in the system, maybe he has a record that you're unaware of."

"Sounds possible. He turned up on my doorstep after all these years, and I invited him into my home with welcoming arms. Well, you would, wouldn't you, if your flesh and blood had gone out of their way to track you down like that? Jesus, I regret the day I opened the front door to him and he announced he was my long-lost son." He shook his head in disbelief.

Sara's heart went out to him. Here was a man, taking the blame for his son's sins. "I've kept something major from you."

He stared at her and inclined his head. "What's that?"

"Your son has pushed the boundaries in the last few hours."

He frowned and scratched the stubble that had erupted on his chin. "Meaning what? What can he do worse than raping and killing three women?"

"He's abducted a police officer. My partner in fact."

He flung himself back in his chair, hard enough to almost tip it over. "What the... damn, I can't say what I really want to say. How do you know this? Has he been in touch? Oh God, don't tell me he's asking the police for a bloody ransom?"

"No, not yet. Although I sense we won't be far away from that." She heaved out a sigh. "He stabbed a victim last night and stole his car. We were at the hospital. The man survived, and Adam showed up there, wielding a knife, trying to find the man. I believe it was his intention to possibly kill him. My partner and I were elsewhere in the building, attending to a different matter, when the alarm was raised. When we got back to A&E, we were told he'd left the building. My partner and I split up in the car park and that's when he must have picked her up."

"Damn." He sat forward again and raked a hand through his hair. "I didn't know he had it in him, to do any of this. I don't know the boy, or should I say, young man, at all. If there's anything I can do to help, I'll willingly do it."

Sara paused to contemplate his words and another idea sparked. "Would you be willing to do a media stint for me?"

"I don't get you?"

"If I can get things arranged, would you speak to him via the media, plead with him to give himself up before it's too late?"

"Of course. If you think he'll listen to me. I have my doubts. I don't know how he ticks. What the hell is he thinking, kidnapping a copper for—?" He stopped talking before he released an expletive which would get him into serious trouble.

"Maybe his intention is to use her as leverage to get you released. I really don't know."

"Perhaps. Let's do it. For his sake as well as your partner's."

"Thanks, I appreciate you trying to help me. I'll get on the blower, but first, I need to clear things with the governor." She glanced up at the officer. "Can you ask her if she has time to see me?"

"I'll need to take him back to his cell first."

"Of course. Shall I wait here? I can make the calls I need to make from here, if the reception is good enough."

"Yep, it should be. I'll be back soon."

The first person Sara called was the press officer, Jane Donaldson. "Jane, it's Sara Ramsey. Sorry to trouble you, I need your expert guidance on a sensitive matter."

"Hi, Inspector, sounds intriguing, how can I be of assistance?"

Sara ran through the predicament she was in and asked for Jane's advice.

"Crikey, I do hope Carla will be all right. Let's see what we can do to get her back to us in one piece. I don't suppose it's going to be possible to get the prisoner here, is it?"

"It's a timing issue. I need to get this plan into action ASAP. I was wondering if you could arrange some of the media to come to the prison and we could do the appeal from here. Of course, I need to run it past the governor first. But I wanted to get in touch with you before I asked her, to ensure it was a feasible task from your end."

"It's doable, I have no doubts about that. I have a couple of journalists in mind who would jump at the chance to have an exclusive, which is probably what it'll need to be in light of the logistics et cetera."

Sara tapped her fingers on the table. "Are we talking press or TV journalists here?"

"A mixture of both. I'm guessing you want the emphasis to be on the TV angle more, yes?"

"Yep. I need the appeal circulated as quickly as possible if we have any significant chance of getting Carla back before he... well, I shouldn't have to spell out to you what this fiend is capable of doing."

"I get that. Leave it with me, I'll see what I can do. Get back to me as soon as you can if the governor gives you the all-clear, okay?"

"Will do. Thanks for this, Jane."

"There's no need to thank me. Let's hope we're successful in our mission and Carla is returned to us unharmed."

"Amen to that. Speak soon." She ended the call and then rang the incident room to apprise the team of the situation. Christine answered the call.

"You must be a mind-reader, I was just about to ring you."

"Sounds ominous. Good news, I hope?"

"Maybe. We've just had a call from the desk sergeant to say a patrol car has spotted the stolen car Zappel is driving."

"And? Tell me they've got him, please."

"The driver lost him. I'm so sorry, boss."

Sara kicked out at the table. "Has Jeff sent more men to the area?"

"He has. He's sure they'll find him again. It was on a small housing estate on the other side of town."

"All right. Keep me updated. I'm in the process of going public with a plea from Jo Zappel to his son. Maybe he'll hear it on the radio and do the right thing, give himself up. If not, perhaps the media attention will be fruitful for us in another way—a member of the public may spot Adam and call us with his whereabouts. As soon as I've sorted out the appeal, I'll be back. I shouldn't be any longer than a couple of hours, although that's going to seem like a lifetime with Carla still missing."

"Okay, boss, I'll let the others know. Good luck."

"Thanks." Sara ended the call and waited for the officer to return. Her mind whirling with questions and what ifs while she sat in the room, staring at the walls that felt like they were closing in on her.

It was another five minutes before the door opened and a smartly dressed woman walked in. She approached Sara with a smile and her hand extended. "It's good to meet you, Inspector Ramsey. I'm Governor Prentice. Officer Gray mentioned you wanted to see me regarding a possible news conference appeal, is that right?"

"It is. Jo Zappel is prepared to do it for us. I've got everything cued up, all I need is the go-ahead from you. Before you say yes or no, ordinarily, I would never put anyone in authority in this predicament, but as you know, these are extenuating circumstances."

"Which is why I'm willing to agree to the media descending upon us. Go ahead and do what you need. If Zappel has given you the all-clear to proceed, then who am I to stand in your way?"

Sara rose from her chair and shook the woman's hand a second time. "It's going to make our lives so much easier, hopefully. I can't thank you enough for agreeing to this, Governor Prentice."

"It's Gemma, and it's also my pleasure. Come with me to my

office, there you can make the necessary calls and I can organise a suitable room to be used. It's all quite exciting really, I've never sanctioned anything along these lines before."

"Let's hope you never have to do it again in the future."

"Fingers crossed. Come with me." Gemma Prentice led Sara through the corridors of the prison in the opposite direction to the way she'd entered. Once they'd reached Gemma's office, they both got to work and arranged everything to go ahead at two that afternoon.

Jane was a superstar and had organised both the BBC and ITV news crews to attend, as well as a couple of local newspapers in the area. She couldn't have asked for more effort to be expended.

All they needed now was for someone out there to provide them with a possible address or location for Adam Zappel, so he could be apprehended.

11

Sara was mentally exhausted by the time the media appeal aired. It had been worth the effort though, because as soon as it was out there, the phones in the incident room began ringing with possible sightings. Sara was almost back at the station when the call came in that Zappel junior had been caught. She smacked her hand on the steering wheel in glee, but that soon dipped when she was told the devastating news that Carla wasn't with him when he was apprehended.

She drove the rest of the way under the siren and arrived at the station not long after a patrol car had brought Zappel in.

Panting, she ran into the station and asked, "Where is he, Jeff?"

He raised a hand. "In a cell, we've processed him. Ma'am, you're going to need to calm down before you see him."

"I don't need you or anyone else telling me what I need to do, Jeff."

"You'd better take it from me, then," an unfamiliar voice cautioned her from the security door that led into the inner sanctum.

Sara whizzed around, ready to give the man a mouthful. "And who the hell are you?"

"Allow me to introduce myself, Inspector Ramsey, I'm DI Des Williams. You were aware of my imminent arrival, were you not?"

Sara nodded and appraised the newcomer. Dressed in a crisp white shirt and dark blue suit. His hair neat and just above his collar. His demeanour oozing authority. She offered a weak smile of friendship. "Yes. Look, I know you're here to take over, but it's my partner we're talking about here."

"All the more reason for you to take a step back, that's the appropriate procedure after all."

Sara sighed. His expression was one of determination. She was knackered; she should have been up for the fight, but what was the point?

"Okay, you win. I'll back down. But can I ask a favour?"

"Like you had an option, anyway. Go ahead, there's no harm in asking."

"Can I be in on the interview with the suspect?" She offered up one of her most dazzling smiles in an effort to get back on his good side.

"Absolutely, categorically, not! N-O-T."

"What? But that's ridiculous. Please, do I have to remind you this is my partner we're talking about?"

"Take it up with your DCI if you're unhappy about the refusal. I have work to do. Time is of the essence after all, right?"

Sara narrowed her eyes and glared at him for a few seconds, the rebuttal she was dying to unleash reverberating around the inside of her mouth. She stormed past him and muttered, "Fucking idiot!"

His laughter followed her up the stairs. "Pleased to meet you too, Inspector."

At the top, she almost bumped into DCI Price. "Sorry, ma'am, I was miles away."

"Is something wrong, Inspector?"

"No. I... oh, what the hell? Yes, everything is wrong. I've busted my gut to get things organised today, and the suspect has been apprehended finally, but the jerk you brought in 'to take over the case' is refusing me access to Zappel." Tears pricked and she let out an exasperated breath.

"While I understand where you're coming from, I need you not to take things personally, Sara. Our priority has to be to get Carla back. You're not in the right frame of mind to tackle the suspect. Look at you! Tell me I'm wrong, if you can."

She turned away and stared at the wall, her shoulders slumped. "Okay, you win." Another idea sparked. "I might not be able to go in there, due to procedures, but there's nothing stopping you being in on the action, is there?"

DCI Price held her arms out to the side. "Where exactly do you think I was going? You never gave me the chance to fill you in. Now, step aside, dear lady, grab yourself a coffee and leave the suspect to the experts."

"Are you suggesting I'm not?"

"Climb down off that damned high horse of yours and stop taking things to heart. I'll let you know how we got on. I'm doing this for you, just remember that the next time you feel like running me down."

Sara gasped. "Not guilty, I never run you down, not to Carla or anyone else come to that."

"Hey, you really have lost your sense of humour today, haven't you?"

Sara turned her back and murmured, "Wouldn't you?"

She walked into the incident room to the applause of her team. She waved the attention away, not exactly overjoyed at how things had developed since her return. "Okay, guys, we have him in custody. While that's brilliant, we need to concentrate our efforts on trying to find out where Carla is. I hate to say this, but I'm going to have to voice my fears. There's every chance we could be looking at a recovery mission. Carla might be dead."

The room fell silent until Marissa tentatively said, "We shouldn't think that way, boss, it's not going to help our cause if we do."

"I know. I'm only trying to be realistic. Let's team up. Craig, get the CCTV footage from all the cameras in the area where he was caught. Between us, we need to trace every step he made since leaving the hospital when he abducted her. Christine, I'll work with you, but first, I need a good dose of caffeine, anyone want to join me?"

They all raised their hands and Christine helped to distribute the cups. "How are you doing?" Christine whispered once they were seated back at her desk.

"Surprisingly well. My heart hurts and I can't shut off thinking something serious has happened to Carla, but I'm also aware how imperative it is to believe she could be safe and well out there."

"That's the spirit. Keep thinking the latter."

"I'm going to do my very best."

*I*t was several hours before DCI Price and DI Williams rejoined the team. "Can I get you both a coffee?" Sara asked, trying to mend some invisible barriers that had been erected since each of them last spoke.

"Thanks, I think we'd both welcome that, Inspector," Carol said. She sank into a nearby chair and said nothing further until Sara had handed her a cup.

"Black for me, no sugar," Williams eventually said.

Sara collected his coffee and placed it on the desk beside the good-looking newcomer. She took up her place close to the chief and asked, "How did it go?"

"Quite well. He was talkative, full of remorse. Not how I expected the interview to go at all." The chief blew on her coffee and took a sip. "After having a brief discussion, once the suspect was returned to his cell, we've come to the conclusion that he didn't abduct Carla."

Sara stared at the chief. "What? I can't believe he's managed to pull the wool over your eyes. Let me interview the bastard. I'll force it out of him if I bloody have to."

"Stop it! Just calm down, Sara, for God's sake. We've been over and over it with him. I believe he's being honest with us when he tells us that he doesn't know where she is," Carol insisted.

"That's utter bullshit. He was at the scene when she went missing, you don't have to be Einstein to figure out what happened. Don't let him dupe you like this, ma'am, please, for Carla's sake."

"I've warned you to calm down, Sara, either that or I'll send you home. You're being disruptive to the investigation and I won't stand for it, do you hear me?"

"Wh... what? Are you serious?" Sara slapped her arms against her thighs and walked into her office where she stood against the door and let the tears of frustration spill. "Jesus! What can I bloody do to make them see sense?"

Carla, if you can hear me, I won't let you down. I'll work day and night to get you back, I swear I will.

The chief and the rest of the team had the sense to leave Sara to dwell in her own self-pity for the next ten minutes. Tears all dried up, she took a cursory look through her post and decided to leave it for another day when she would be in a better frame of mind to deal with it. She rang Mark, needing to hear a friendly voice. "Hi, can you talk?"

"Of course. Hey, you sound down in the dumps. What's up, darling?"

"I'm not feeling my best, it's been a super crappy day."

"Sorry to hear that. Anything I can do to make things better for you?"

"I wish. Umm... I wasn't going to tell you this, but Carla was abducted this morning."

"Jesus... Bloody hell, I don't know what to say, sweetheart. Who took her, do you know?"

"We have a rough idea. We've caught the bastard, but frustratingly he's denying it. I'm not allowed near the suspect because of protocol. Five minutes in a sodding room with me and I'd force the information out of him."

"That's so wrong. You should be able to question him, you have that right, don't you?"

"No. Because Carla is my partner, there would be a conflict of interest. I'm bereft, just hanging around here, not knowing what to do next. I know everyone says this when a partner is no longer beside them, but I honestly feel like my right arm has been cut off."

"I'm sorry, it must be hard for you. I hope she's safe. Can't you torture the bastard to get the information out of him?"

"Sadly not. As much as I'd like to set up a rack and other equipment of that ilk, it's against the law."

"Ah, right, silly me."

"Don't worry, we'll sort it, eventually. I just needed to hear your voice. I feel a whole lot better now, love. Thank you."

"Sara, I'm always here for you, you know that."

Her heart fluttered. "I know, that's why I fell in love with you."

"Don't you ever forget how much I love you."

"I won't. I'd better get back to it now. I'm feeling more energised at least, ready to go into battle again for the umpteenth time today."

"Stay positive, my brave little warrior. I'll say a silent prayer for Carla and hope she comes back to us soon. See you later. Ring me if you're going to be late."

"I will. I'll probably hang around until sevenish, if the new inspector in charge will allow it."

"You didn't tell me someone has taken over from you. Christ, no wonder you're feeling down. Sorry, love. I'm sure it's for the best."

"Yeah, I know it is. It still sucks, though. See you later. Love you."

"Stay strong. Love you back."

She ended the call and stared out at the clouds drifting past, covering up the vivid blue sky in a patchwork of fluffiness. She remained that way, her thoughts with her absent partner for the next five minutes, until the phone on her desk rang.

"DI Sara Ramsey, how can I help?"

"Hi, I was put through to you because of the issue that has just been raised."

"Sorry? Who is this?"

"Captain Potts from the Hereford Fire Brigade. I believe we've met once or twice in the past few months."

"Ah, yes. Of course. What can I do for you, Captain?"

"Umm… something happened here a few minutes ago. As we have a loose connection, I thought it would be best coming direct to you."

"Why don't you tell me what happened?"

"One of our men got taken," he replied bluntly.

"Excuse me? What do you mean?"

"You heard me, one of my men has been abducted. Right before our bloody eyes and there wasn't a damn thing we could do about it either. We tried, I swear we did, but it was pointless."

"Okay, let's go over this again. Who was taken?"

"Gary Charlton, I believe he used to go out with your partner, didn't he? They split up a few months ago, if my memory serves me right."

Sara's heart dropped into her stomach. *Shit!* "That's right. Okay, are you still at the station?"

"Yes, I'll be here all evening."

"I'm on my way. Don't move until I get there." Sara tore out of her chair and entered the incident room. "Shit! We've got it wrong. Carla wasn't abducted by Zappel at all. Fuck, fuck, fuck!" Her team stopped what they were doing and stared at her, one or two of them frowning at each other. "Will and Craig, come with me. Shit, I'm sorry, my head is spinning. I know I'm not making any sense. Brief rundown and then we have to fly. Gary, Carla's ex, has just been abducted. I believe this has something to do with Carla getting beaten up a few weeks ago. Whoever did this has now got both of them. He was taken from the fire station. I'm going over there now to get further details."

Inspector Williams walked into the room. He stood by the door, his arms folded across his broad chest, listening. Sara stared at him as she issued orders to her team. "Get the footage from the fire station, they must have cameras on site. Circulate the reg number of the vehicle. We'll be back soon."

Sara headed towards Williams. He remained where he was, blocking her path.

"Not so fast, Inspector. I demand to know what's going on here."

"Please, you have to let me go. Come with me if you must, but we're wasting time. I can fill you in on the way. Please, I need to do this. Put yourself in my shoes. This is tearing me apart, not being out there looking for her."

He heaved out a sigh and relented. "We'll take my car, you're in no fit state to drive."

"Okay. And thank you. Will and Craig, you go in a separate car. It'll be better if we have two vehicles out there, just in case."

The four of them raced out of the building. Sara shouted to Jeff on the way through, "Get every available patrol vehicle to assist us, Jeff. I'll take the flack for it if any comes your way."

"Already actioned, ma'am. Good luck."

Des Williams started the engine of his Ford Mondeo while Sara slipped into the passenger side and hooked up her seatbelt. "You're not one of these boy racer types, are you?"

"Nope. You're safe with me."

He revved the engine, looked both ways and put his foot down. He screeched out of the car park, flinging Sara's head back in the process. "You think," she muttered.

"No boy racer, but I'm the adult version, whatever that might be called. You're safe. I've taken my advanced driving course. You're going to need to give me directions, what with this not being my patch."

Sara nodded and gripped the door handle with one hand and the edge of her seat with the other.

He laughed. "I take it you don't believe me."

"Evidence proves the opposite is true. Take a right and then the next left up ahead. Crap, I hope I can remember the way, Carla's usually the one shouting out the directions for me to follow."

His tone turned serious once more. "We'll get her. You'd better fill me in on what you know on the way."

"Okay. Last month, Gary, who has just been abducted, who is Carla's former boyfriend, was causing problems. No, wait, I'm leaving out a crucial part. One day, at the end of last month, Carla showed up at work after being beaten up on her doorstep. She was out cold, a neighbour found her late at night."

"All right, what's this got to do with the boyfriend? You suspect he was to blame for the GBH?"

"I didn't at first, and Carla was adamant he wasn't involved. As a precaution, I went round there to warn him off, just in case. I pulled up at the end of my shift, was about to step out of the car when a bloke approached him. They had words, shall we say, and the stranger jabbed him in the stomach. I let the bloke go and then got out of the car to tackle Gary about it. He was shocked to see me there. Shocked and embarrassed, I suppose. I asked him what was going on. He denied anything was. Then it clicked that his confrontation probably had something to do with what had happened to Carla." She sighed and shook her head. "I should have been more forceful, got the bloody truth out of him."

"He denied knowing about it, I take it."

"Yep. Told me to butt out of something that didn't concern me."

"And what did Carla say when you told her?" Des asked.

Sara fell silent.

"Shit! You haven't told her, have you? Ah, I get it, now she's gone missing, that's why you're feeling the way you are; you're riddled with guilt," Des summed it up perfectly.

"Thanks for pointing out the obvious. Wouldn't you be if you were in my situation?"

"Nope. Because I would never allow myself to get in that situation in the first place. I would have pinned him up against the wall by the throat and forced the bloody truth out of him, to save all this kicking off the way it has."

"Hindsight is a wonderful thing," she murmured.

"Ain't that the truth? So, who do you think is behind the abductions?"

"I don't know. I didn't really get a good enough look at the bloke to do some extra digging on the side. His intentions were clear towards Gary and if he's the one who beat Carla up, well, he's either an idiot or a hard piece of shit who doesn't give two hoots about jumping on a copper."

"Which do you think is the most likely?"

"I dread to think is my honest answer. God, I hope I haven't messed things up, in more ways than one. If Carla ever finds out that I had an inkling Gary was in trouble and didn't tell her, she'll want to string me up from the nearest tree."

"I doubt it. If we find her, her first reaction is going to be one of relief."

"And her second?" Sara turned and asked.

"Let's cross that bridge when we come to it. Where next?"

"Sorry. Yes, another two right turns and we should be almost there."

Sara's mobile rang. She fished it out of her pocket. "Hi, Christine, what have you got?"

"Good news I think, boss."

"Wait, let me put the phone on speaker. Right, go ahead. We're listening."

"Two patrol cars are in pursuit of the van which we identified swooping in to abduct Gary. They're chasing it on the other side of the town. They're currently out at Withington, heading on the A4103 towards Worcester."

"Going towards my patch," Des added.

"All right, Christine, we'll head out that way, see if we can help. Can you make Will and Craig aware of the situation? They're following us, but just in case we lose them in traffic, as it's quite heavy at present."

"I'll do that now. Good luck, boss. If I hear anything else, I'll get in touch."

"Thanks."

Sara ended the call and braced herself for the high-speed chase she guessed was ahead of them.

"Hang on tight." Des flicked the siren on and floored the accelerator.

"Already actioned. You will be careful, won't you?"

"Of course. That's my middle name... not!" He smirked and turned to face her.

"Please, keep your eyes on the road. I'd like to get out of this alive, if at all possible."

He snorted. "What, so your partner can string you up?"

"Ha-bloody-ha. Just get us there in one piece."

. . .

"That's okay, Christine. I was going to get in touch with you later, anyway. How's it going? Any news on who the kidnapper was?"

"Yes, he's a notorious loan shark in the area. Paul 'Pitbull' Rogers."

"Oh, great. If you were introduced to a man by that name, would you bloody do business with him?"

"Nope. I'd run a mile. On the other hand, I suppose it depends how deep you are into debt and how desperate you are at the time."

"Yeah, there is that. You know Carla's back with Gary, don't you?"

"I'd heard. Does she know that Gary's involvement with the deceased is the reason she was attacked?"

"No. I don't have it in me to tell her, not yet. I know I should have, but... the opportunity has passed us by now. Can you tell the rest of the team to keep schtum about it? I know it's not an ideal situation, but until I can come up with a solution, my hands are tied."

"Don't worry, I'll pre-warn the rest of the team. Gary will show his true colours again soon, once the romance has died down again and the reality hits home. He must be up to his neck in debt. I'm sure that will put an extra burden on their relationship."

"You could be right. We all need to be there to offer Carla our support when the inevitable happens. Going back to the cases we were dealing with, have the families been informed the suspect has been apprehended?"

"They have, I made the calls myself. They were all relieved and asked me to pass on their thanks and best wishes."

"That's what makes our job worthwhile at the end of the day."

"It does indeed. I'll go now. See you tomorrow."

"Thanks for the update. Take care, Christine."

Sara ended the call and hugged Misty, who inched herself out of her arms a few minutes later. "I'd better get to the shops. We have Mum and Dad coming to lunch on Sunday and nothing in the fridge or freezer."

She trailed around the supermarket in a daze, picking up a large joint of beef and a packet of Aunt Bessie's Yorkshire puddings as she passed the frozen food section.

On the drive home, with her boot full of food, she reflected on how lucky she was not to have any angst or concerns in her life, none that matched the extent of which Carla was dealing with, anyway. Well, except the onerous task of getting rid of a member of her team, but that could wait until the deadline drew closer.

Enough about work, life was good in the Ramsey household. In fact, all things considered, life was too good; she crossed her fingers hoping that didn't change anytime in the near future. She'd had her share of heartbreak in the past. Now it was time for her to sit back and be happy for a change.

THE END

*T*hank you for reading Indefensible - Sara and Carla are due to return in the gripping **LOCKED AWAY** - When the past catches up with the present...

... the result can be deadly.

erhaps you'd also consider reading another of my most popular series? Grab the first book in the Justice series here, CRUEL JUSTICE

Or the gritty first book in the Hero Series TORN APART.

If you've enjoyed this book please consider leaving a review or possibly telling a friend.

*T*hank you.

KEEP IN TOUCH WITH M A COMLEY

Pick up a FREE novella by signing up to my newsletter today.
https://BookHip.com/WBRTGW

BookBub
www.bookbub.com/authors/m-a-comley

Blog
http://melcomley.blogspot.com

Join my special Facebook group to take part in monthly giveaways.

Readers' Group

Printed in Great Britain
by Amazon

81264708R00111